Tom Gillies.

TOM GILLIES;

THE KNOTS HE TIED AND UNTIED.

BY
MRS. GEORGE GLADSTONE.

Lamplighter Publishing
Waverly, PA 18471

Tom Gillies.

Copyright © 2002 by Mark Hamby
All rights reserved.
First Printing, May, 2003

Published by Lamplighter Publishing; a division of
Cornerstone Family Ministries, Inc.

The Lamplighter Rare Collector's Series is a series
of Christian family literature from the 17th, 18th,
19th, & 20th centuries. Each edition is printed in an
attractive hard-bound collector's format. For more
information, write: Lamplighter Publishing, P.O.
Box 777, Waverly, PA 18471 or call 1-888-A-
GOSPEL.

Author: Mrs. George Gladstone
Printed by Jostens in the United States of America
Arrestox 53500, Gold M842, black

ISBN: 1-58474-048-5

PREFACE.

Tom Gillies was generous, passionate, mischievous, and easily led. He had so often been in the wrong that his father and mother looked upon him as the black sheep of the family, and never gave him credit for doing well. He had established a reputation as a worthless vagabond on Norton Island. His mother continually warned him that Dick Potter would be his ruin at last.

Each day they would meet at their favorite cave at the edge of the cliff, concoct their plans for the day and plot mischievous schemes which gained them so bad a name on the island.

But Tom soon learns that bad habits will fasten strong chains around him, and sin will tie knots in the cords that bind him, making him a prisoner. He discovers how these knots can be unfastened by the One who is at hand to help him. Now all Tom needs is the courage to say no to his "friend" Dick and follow the true Friend who will untie those dreadful knots, and free him to live a productive life among the people of Norton Island.

TOM GILLIES.

CHAPTER I.

TOM IS INTRODUCED.

NORTON ISLAND was two miles and a half from the pretty watering-place of Dixtown; it was a point of interest to visitors to the latter place, who enjoyed sailing across the bay to picnic there, when the day was calm and the sun shone brightly. It had lofty cliffs, which terminated here and there in abrupt points, deep caves, and picturesque coves. The view from the back of the island commanded a wide expanse of ocean, and was so wild that the seabirds built their nests in the crannies of the rock, choosing such dangerous places that only daring lads like Tom Gillies and his friend Dick Potter attempted to plunder them of their eggs.

One large mansion and farm, belonging to Mr. Pender, the proprietor of the limestone quarries, and the cottages where the people who worked for him and a few fishermen dwelt, made up the sum of the habitations on Norton Island, save the schoolhouse, where an old spinster lived rent-free. She was a fairly-educated woman, who had once served in Mr. Pender's family, and that gentleman allowed her an annual stipend for teaching the children of the men he employed.

Norton Island was rather celebrated for its limestone quarries. Many vessels anchored in the roadstead during the year, waiting for cargo, whilst it also afforded a harbor in time of storm. It boasted no place of worship; occasionally divine service was held in the schoolroom on Sunday afternoon, and in that case a great bell sounded for half an hour before it commenced, in order to summon the villagers.

The Gillies family, with the exception of the eldest daughter Sally, turned a deaf ear to the call. Mrs. Gillies contended that Sunday was designed for poor people to spend in idleness. "We work right away for six days," she said, "and it's hard if we can't rest on the seventh."

Certainly she was an industrious woman so far as the concerns of this world were involved; but she had to learn that honoring God was paramount, and that, if she served Him, she would better fulfil her duties to her family, and to all mankind.

Mr. Gillies had lived on Norton Island for twenty-five years. He settled there soon after his marriage, and had worked in the limestone quarries ever since. He had a hard struggle to live while his children were young, but when our story opens, his four eldest sons helped substantially to maintain the home. They rented the cottage adjoining their father's; and though the eldest, Harry, was soon to be married, the other three were doing so well, they intended occupying it as before.

It was customary for the women to sell prawns in Dixtown. When Sally Gillies was old enough to cook the dinner, her mother undertook this business, and rather enjoyed the many journeys to and from Norton Island it entailed.

One beautiful afternoon in August she returned home after having disposed of her basket of prawns satisfactorily. She was particularly happy over her day's work, for two reasons:—the first was, that she had sold her fish well; and the second, that she had made an arrangement for one of her sons.

"I've been and gone and done it, Tom," she said, as she entered the cottage and threw down her basket.

"Done what?" questioned a boy of fourteen, who was standing idly by the window.

"Got you a situation," answered his mother. 'To-morrow-week you go to Miss Pringle. You'll have to run errands, clean out the shop, and look after the bakehouse, and, what's more, have done with your idle, vagabond habits. You're no good to your father nor me, we can't do nothing with you. You won't work regular at any time, and Dick Potter will be your ruin at last. He does his duty sometimes, but you never will stick to anything but catching crabs and hunting the rocks."

"What's Miss Pringle going to give Tom, mother?" asked Sally, a girl of sixteen, who was darning a coarse sock.

"He's to have his board for the first six months, and afterwards she'll give him a shilling a week besides; and she says, Tom, you may come home now and then of a Saturday night, and back again of a Sunday night, when the boys have the boat convenient; I'm sure you ought to be glad to have another chance; and you may thank Miss Pringle for taking you, when she knows well enough what a troublesome fellow she'll have to deal with."

"I'd just as soon be a baker's boy as stay here to be found fault with by you and father," answered Tom, sullenly. "Nobody thinks I can do right. I'm sure I'd stick to the prawning or quarrying if you'd let me; but there's too many at home, and you want to get rid of me."

"That's not true, lad," said Mr. Gillies, a tall, rough-looking man, who entered the room at this moment. "You know you won't work steadily, and that it all ends in talk with you. Dick Potter will ruin you, and you will ruin him; and the sooner you're separated the better. I'm quite tired of hearing complaints from one and the other; this island is too small to hold two such boys. I'm glad for you to go away; if any one can manage you, Miss Pringle can."

"I ain't no worse than others, father," replied Tom. "I'd do better if you'd be kind to me. I never was a favorite at home, and never shall be. Sally is the only one who ever speaks civilly to me. Ask her if I'm a bad brother to her."

Mrs. Gillies glanced at her daughter, but as the latter made no reply, she continued the conversation.

"Your father speaks as he finds you, Tom," she said. "Even Mr. Pender has given you up; he thinks you'll behave better among strangers; and yet he's promised to take Dick Potter on, the first opening that comes."

"And so he may for all I care," muttered the boy. "I'm ready to be off to Miss Pringle to-morrow if you like. I'm sure, with such a lot of children about, there isn't much to make me want to stay here."

"You're an ungrateful rascal," said Mr. Gillies; and the lad would have received a heavy blow, had he not twisted round and made good his retreat through the open door.

Tom was not far wrong when he said there were too many at home for comfort. Mr. and Mrs. Gillies had eleven children. Harry and Will, the two eldest, were fishermen, and owned a boat between them. Ned and James worked with their father in the limestone quarries; Sally came next, then Tom, and five young children.

Tom ran as fast as his legs would carry him until he reached the edge of the cliff, then he scrambled down to a favorite cave, where he and Dick Potter had concocted their plans for many a day, and plotted mischievous schemes which gained for these boys so bad a name on the island. Tom under different training would have been a better boy. He was extremely generous, very passionate, intensely mischievous, and easily led. Dick Potter, on the other hand, had no redeeming qualities; he excited Tom to acts of daring which the latter would not have thought of, and he always took care to be on the safe side himself.

Tom had so often been in the wrong that his father and mother looked upon him as the black sheep of the family, and never gave him credit for doing well. The boy hardened under this treatment, and grew reckless. To his sister Sally he was rarely rude or unkind; but her character was scarcely matured enough to guide him, though she did her best to induce her brother to relinquish any wild scheme that came to her knowledge, and would, she knew, bring him into punishment if carried out.

Tom sat in the cave and threw pebbles into the water; the tide was rising so that he could not search after crabs, and unless Dick came soon he would have to abandon his position, for the water rolled so nearly up to him. In fact, he was on the point of retreating, when a long low whistle announced that his companion was near.

"You're later than usual, Dick," called out Tom.

"You mean you're earlier."

"Well, I suppose I am. There ain't much to tempt me to stay at home. Now I remember, I came without my tea. But Sally will look after me. I've got something to tell you, Dick."

"Well, speak up; what is it?"

"First, let's get out of our cave to higher ground; the tide's coming in."

The boys scrambled on to a jutting point of rock—another favorite place they had—and sat down again.

"What's up?" asked Dick.

"I'm going to live with Miss Pringle. I shall have to help in the bakehouse, run errands, and sweep out the shop."

Dick whistled.

"What do you think of it?" asked Tom.

"Why, that you won't be there a month. Miss Pringle's a dreadfully difficult woman to please, I've heard."

"Anything is better than staying at home," said Tom.

"I don't' think so," replied Dick.

"It's different with you and me. I'm not wanted here; and though the bakehouse will be hot after so much fresh air, I'd rather be stewed than told every minute in the day that I'm a good-for-nothing fellow."

"You will never stay, I tell you."

"Is that all you have to say, Dick? You ain't a bit sorry I'm going," said Tom, as if hurt at his companion's carelessness.

"Of course I'm sorry. I shall lose my best friend," replied Dick; "and mind, Tom, I shall always be ready to help you. And now we won't talk any more about your leaving Norton Island, for there's to be a splendid shooting at the quarry in half an hour. Let's go over and watch it."

The boys started at once, and were in time to see a great blasting of the rock, which generally

took place when most of the men had finished
their day's work.

CHAPTER II.

MOTHER CRAMPTON.

MOTHER CRAMPTON had passed her seventy-seventh birthday, and it seemed probable she would live to be ninety or more, for her steps were elastic and her eyes bright. She was a well-known inhabitant of Dixtown, having rented the same two rooms for more than thirty years. She kept a small shop, and sold boxes of beautiful shells, which were collected from the neighboring sands by a gentleman who had seen better days, and who earned in this manner a bare subsistence for himself and daughter.

Mother Crampton was diminutive in stature, but neat and trim in person. She wore a dress of coarse material, and a dark brown woolen apron. Sometimes both dress and apron were patched in many places, and not always with the same-colored stuff; but the stitches were so small, and the turnings so even, they but served to show how thrifty she was, and what her still nimble fingers were able to perform. They moved quickly, too, when the old dame knitted her black stockings. How she managed to walk about in her heavy, thick leather boots was a question that she decided by many ominous shakes of the head, and a long explanation about the needs-be of women so far advanced in life as she was trying to keep clear of rheumatism.

Though Mother Crampton's face was wrinkled, and the lines in it deep-set, she was pleasant-looking and intelligent, with a placid expression which denoted a mind at rest. She was very peaceful and contented, because she trusted in God, and had found the joy of believing in Jesus for many a long year; nor was she ashamed to confess her Saviour before men.

We have said that Mother Crampton rented two rooms. That on the ground-floor was her shop and parlor, overhead was her bedroom, which was somewhat encumbered by a full-sized, four-post bed, covered with a patchwork quilt, sewn by herself.

The lower room had a curious medley of furniture of all sorts in it. The kitchen fireplace was let into a recess. The three shelves over it were filled with pans, irons, candlesticks, and a great variety of cooking utensils. Near to this recess there was a small wooden cupboard, in which four dozen cups and saucers, six earthen ware teapots, and as many small jugs and sugar basins, were kept.

Opposite to it stood a chest of drawers, which held the good dame's Sunday clothes, and all the linen and wearing apparel she possessed, except her black silk bonnet, which was carefully pinned up in a pocket handkerchief and deposited in a square box under her bed. A great variety of articles were displayed on the top of the chest of drawers, which was protected from scratches by a green baize cloth. Among them was an old Bible, full of quaint pictures, and a shell-house which served for a barometer. It contained two wooden figures fastened together by catgut. "Let my old woman appear," said Mother Crampton, "and I'm sure the weather will be fine; and the rain will fall if her husband shows himself."

A small, round, wooden table was placed next to the drawers. On it were piled, one above the other, four boxes filled with shells, which were carefully wrapped in paper to protect them from the dust. By their side stood a large pair of shells.

The lowest shelf was much wider than the other two; it contained packets of blacklead, bottles of ink, a cup of oatmeal, onions, pipes, lumps of salt, lucifers, a few prawns, and sometimes a bunch of parsley or mint. The walls of the room were adorned with brown paper bags filled with spearmint, sage, and other dried herbs, while three portraits, cut out of black paper, and intended to be likenesses of dear friends, hung over the chest of drawers.

Mother Crampton was very busy about three o'clock on the day after our story commences. She folded up her work at half-past two, set the cups and saucers on the wooden table, put the kettle on the fire, and took a loaf of bread and a small piece of butter out of the corner cupboard. Whoever ate a thick slice of bread and butter paid an extra halfpenny, and at the same rate for every additional slice.

The kettle was singing and hissing when Mrs. Gillies entered, looking very much heated.

"How do you do, mother?" she said. "I'm glad to sit down a bit; it's been very hot to-day."

"Have you had a good morning's trade?" asked the old dame. "You haven't many prawns left, I see."

"I've been uncommon lucky, considering I came over later than usual," answered Mrs. Gillies; "and, what's better, I've got rid of all my stale fish. I put a tidy lot at the bottom of my basket, and a young lady on the terrace bought them all."

"Did you pass them off as fresh?"

Mrs. Gillies laughed. "Of course I did, mother. I said too, 'You may trust me, Miss.' All's fair in Dixtown; no one takes advantage of the other."

"And she believed you and bought your prawns! O, neighbor! When will you learn to do unto others as you would be done by?"

"I've my living to get, and a large family to feed and clothe; it won't do to be too particular," answered Mrs. Gillies.

"You may prosper, or think you prosper, by falsehood," said the dame; "but it will never last. Honesty is the best policy, both for this world and the next."

"Don't preach, mother," replied Mrs. Gillies, good-humoredly. "I've had a capital day's trade, and I'm very happy; besides, I'm too hot to listen to a sermon."

"Neighbor, neighbor! I wish you wouldn't talk like that. Remember that your actions are known to God, and that you will one day have to render an account to him for all your false dealings."

"Hush, hush! good mother; you're too much of a saint for me. Now, listen. I've some news for you. Our Tom's going to live with Miss Pringle, and I hope you'll give him a kind word now and then."

Dame Crampton was about to answer, when two other women entered the room, and the conversation became more general. There was a strong smell of tea very soon, and many confidences were exchanged in the next quarter of an hour, to which the old mother listened with a grave face. She could not jest with her customers over what she considered dishonest dealings. Sometimes she ventured to remonstrate, but her words were not much heeded; still she persisted in bearing her testimony to what she believed to be the truth.

CHAPTER III.

MISS PRINGLE AND HER LODGERS.

MISS PRINGLE kept a small baker's shop in Dixtown, and carried on a brisk trade; in fact, she was rather noted for her home-made bread. The appearance of her shop from without did not betoken much business, for the window was small, and had nothing in it but a loaf, a few stale cakes, and a half-a-dozen bottles filled with acidulated drops, peppermint and ginger lozenges, barley-sugar sticks, and bull's eyes.

Behind the shop was the staircase; then came the kitchen. On the floor above were two good rooms, and a smaller one which went over part of the long passage that ran through the house into the garden.

It was a most productive piece of ground; the air of Dixtown was so mild that all kinds of fruits and vegetables throve, while fuchias and myrtles flourished out of doors all the winter, and geraniums needed no greenhouse to protect them from frost.

Beyond the kitchen was the bakehouse, where Miss Pringle might be seen every morning at six o'clock kneading her dough, for she was by no means an idle woman; she managed to conduct her business with the help of a boy, who attended to the oven, swept out the shop, and carried bread round to her customers.

Miss Pringle was a tall, thin, spare woman. It was difficult to determine her age. Some said she was fifty, others sixty; but no one ventured to ask the question, "How old are you?" and she was never heard to mention any circumstance which afforded information on the subject.

She made no friends, and rarely invited any of her customers beyond the shop. Not a single inhabitant of Dixtown had ever entered her bedroom; she invariably kept the door locked, and carried the key in her pocket. This circumstance excited no suspicion in the neighborhood, for she was considered very eccentric, and it was looked upon as part of her eccentricity. The real truth of the matter was this—she was a miser, and secreted her gold up stairs. When the house-door was closed to customers at nine o'clock in summer, and eight in winter, and the boy sent to his bed under the staircase, Miss Pringle began to enjoy herself. She retired to her bedroom, and, fearing no intruders, counted her money ere she fell asleep.

On the day before we make her acquaintance she had realized the sum of two hundred pounds, which she kept in a stocking within a small wooden box, secured by a padlock. For a long time she moved this box about her room, never being satisfied that she had chosen the safest place for it. During the last few weeks she had adopted a new plan, and placed it inside a bandbox, which she put on the top shelf of a large cupboard that faced the bedroom door.

"That bandbox will not excite attention if any misfortune overtakes me, and I am obliged to let any one in here," she said to herself over and over again by way of encouragement.

Miss Pringle never laughed heartily; she could smile faintly, but that was all. It mattered not what conversation was held, nor what jokes were indulged in, her face ever wore the same unmoved expression.

She was civil, attentive, and anxious to please her customers, but, as we have said, she made no friends, nor did she wish for any.

She kept a most parsimonious table. Twice a week she dined off fresh dripping and bread, and three times off bacon and potatoes; while every Sunday she had a small joint of mutton, which served for Monday too.

No boy ever remained with Miss Pringle beyond six months. She promised Mrs. Gillies that Tom should have one shilling a week if he stayed half-a-year in her service, and she was satisfied to make this bargain, for, judging from past experience, no lad pleased her so much as to involve the payment of weekly wages.

Before we tell how Tom Gillies arrived at his first situation, and entered on his new duties, we must speak of the lodger, who, with his only child, occupied the front room over the shop and smaller one over the passage, for which Miss Pringle charged three shillings a week.

His name was Newton. He was a widower, and a great invalid. Every one in Dixtown who knew him treated him with marked respect, even though his clothes were shabby and his coat threadbare. There was no mystery about his early history; it was just a simple every-day one, of a man who had never been successful, and who had no good friend to advance his interests.

Mr. Newton lost his wife at the birth of his daughter Annie, and about the same time his health, which was before so good, declined, and he had to contend with disease and pain. He was not quite penniless when he came to

Dixtown two years before our story opens, and selected it as a place of residence because he had a letter of introduction to a gentleman there, and was ordered by the hospital doctor to live in a sheltered spot by the sea. He never presented his letter, for his ailments did not admit of his undertaking regular work.

Soon after Mr. Newton and his daughter, who had just completed her fourteenth year, were established in their lodgings, an idea struck him, and one which he hoped, if carried out, would afford him a means of subsistence. He was a conchologist, and had suited that branch of natural history for his own amusement. Dixtown at low water was rich in shells, so he determined to collect the rarest specimens, and name and arrange them in boxes for sale. In his boyish days, and long before he felt the pressure of care, he had done this for amusement.

It took him some weeks of hard study to master the names of the various specimens of shells he found on the shore, and then he fell seriously ill. Just at this crisis, and when his little hoard of money was exhausted, his only relative in the world died and left him fifty pounds. This sum was a great boon to the poor man, who was no longer haunted by the dread of starvation which must have come but for this timely aid.

Many days passed before Mr. Newton was well enough to resume his search after shells; during this time his little daughter nursed him tenderly. She was old for her years and clever too. Her father, who was no mean scholar, carried on her education, and she eagerly learned of him. "You must be a governess, so be diligent, child," he said. And Annie was diligent; for she loved her father devotedly, and to please him gave her the purest joy she knew. She was so anxious to lighten his cares, and be of some use, that she tried to understand what shells he required for his collections, and during his illness spent many hours alone in searching after rare specimens.

Mr. Newton was obliged to purchase several expensive books of reference. "It is not money quite lost," he said to his daughter; "you may turn them into shillings hereafter, and I must be competent myself if I am to be an authority for others."

It was a happy day for them when the first box of shells was completed. It was made of card-board, and had a glass lid. Inside were two layers of shells, which were tastefully arranged in trays on pink and white wool. The upper layer contained five trays; in each tray were twenty-four different kinds of shells. The lower layer held the large single shells; the tiniest sorts were gummed on black paper. Annie, who watched her father's operations carefully, so that she might render him assistance when the second box was arranged, was delighted with the success of this first attempt. So soon as the final touches were put, the question—which had many times been discussed—as to who should sell the boxes, had to be decided.

"Do not ask Miss Pringle," said Annie; "she will be sure to want half the money we get. I have seen a little shop just off the High Street, and a tiny old woman standing at the door; her name is Crampton; let us call on her. It is a good situation for our purpose; the visitors must pass on their way to the fishmarket, the pier, and the south sands."

Dixtown was by no means a large place, and most of the shops were in the High Street; but Annie was right in the reasons she gave, when she suggested that Mother Crampton was the best person to find a market for the boxes.

Mr. Newton had no difficulty in coming to terms with the old dame. "It's not a good time for selling, sir," she said, hanging up the paper he brought with him that invited visitors to inspect the shells. "We've but few strangers in the town now."

Nevertheless, in four days a purchaser came, who gave the guinea that Mr. Newton asked; and as Mother Crampton was satisfied with one shilling commission, and the materials cost but two, he made a handsome profit on the transaction.

Annie and her father were overjoyed. This success gave them an impetus to go forward; and when a letter came from London ordering two more boxes at the same price, their hearts were full of gratitude.

Before the next season Mr. Newton had a good stock in hand, which sold so well that he felt satisfied this new business would enable him to live comfortably, though sparingly, and pay his landlady regularly. To be sure, Miss Pringle's apartments were not spacious, but they sufficed for himself and daughter; for Annie occupied the tiny room over the passage, and her father slept on an old sofa in the front room.

Annie was a busy little maiden, and a careful housekeeper. She cooked nicely, and could buy to the best advantage. Her knowledge had come early; because she was motherless and had an invalid father, she was obliged to forego the pleasures which children of her age love best.

For some months all went smoothly, and then a fresh calamity threatened Mr. Newton. He had felt his eyesight failing since his last severe illness, and had a presentiment he might one day be blind. He could not help dwelling on this fear sometimes. When he was depressed

Annie roused him by her cheerful words, and reminded him that God did not forget them. She and her father were not formal believers, but recognized the wise Hand that overruled all the events of their lives.

The young girl found a true friend in Mother Crampton. On the morning after Mrs. Gillies had informed the kind old lady that her son Tom was going to live with Miss Pringle, she took a large box of shells to her for sale. Her heart was heavy, for her father had said, "Annie, my eyes are so weak to-day I will lie down and rest them, while you carry the case we finished yesterday to Mother Crampton."

"Do, father," she answered, "and do not be worried. I know most of the shells by name, and can find some of the sorts quite easily. If you can see well enough to make the boxes, we shall get along all right."

But, in spite of her words, she felt an inward chill when she thought, "What will become of us if papa goes blind?"

Annie was a special favorite of Mother Crampton's. "I'm so glad to see you, dear, for I've just sold my last box, and I've an order for another from the same gentleman," she said, as the young girl entered her shop.

"O, mother! How pleased I am! My father will be quite happy to hear it. He is very dull to-day, his eyes seem so weak."

"He must see through you, child. He will miss the beautiful scenes in God's world at first, but he won't be blind in that other world. The New Jerusalem will be far grander than this, and yet I'm told by them that have gone to foreign parts there isn't often a fairer scene to be met with than ours."

"Papa says the view from the cliff, which takes in the beautiful bay and castle-hill, with Norton Island beyond, and dear little St. Helen's, is a perfect picture; and he knows something about other lands, for he used to travel when he was young, and he visited many grand cities."

"How is Miss Pringle, Annie?" asked Mother Crampton, turning the conversation abruptly into another channel.

"All well as usual. Why do you ask?"

"Because I hear she is going to have a new boy named Tom Gillies. I've known his mother a long time. I'm afraid he's not very steady. Try and do him good, my dear; his mother doesn't love God, and I pity a boy that hasn't praying parents."

"He will not stay long with Miss Pringle. She has had three boys during the last month," said Annie.

"How do you manage to lodge with her if she's so particular?"

"We pay our rent regularly, and that is all she requires," answered the young girl, smiling. "I think if papa were to become blind, and we failed in our weekly payments, she would be neither kind nor civil," she added, with a sigh.

"Don't anticipate trouble, my child; have faith in God when the rain falls as well as when the sun shines. He doesn't forget His children. You're growing older every day, and will soon be able to make the boxes alone; and if I can sell them, you can keep the wolf from the door even if your father's eyesight fails. Here's the sovereign I owe you."

Annie left her friend holding the sovereign tightly in one hand. She had no great distance to go before she reached home, scarcely a quarter of a mile. She walked by the side of some iron railings which were placed at the edge of the cliff, and stopped when she came to a gate that led by a narrow pathway down to the sands. Here a seat was placed, and she could not resist sitting down to admire the scene. The beautiful bay lay at her feet; to the north were a range of thickly-wooded cliffs; in the far distance were sloping hills covered with well-cultivated fields, and on the right rose the castle-hill.

"It makes a pretty picture," Annie said aloud.

"It does, dearest."

She turned, and found her father had joined her. "What news do you bring?" he asked.

"Very good indeed. Here is a sovereign. The box I took to-day is sold too."

"Thank God for that!" answered Mr. Newton. "O, Annie! if I could but see clearly, how happy I should be! But the scene grows so misty. Pray for me, that I may be patient if what I dread so much comes to pass."

CHAPTER IV.

TOM AND DICK GO FOR A HOLIDAY.

TOM made up his mind he would have one holiday with Dick Potter before he was "harnessed up," as he called it, to Miss Pringle. Mrs. Gillies did not encourage her son to do his best at his first situation; she rather gave him a distaste for it. Every word that Tom uttered which displeased her made her shake her head, and say tauntingly, "You'll learn to speak to your elders differently, young gentleman, when Miss Pringle has you in hand." So Tom did not try to do better; he made himself, if possible, more disagreeable; he pulled his little brothers' hair, disturbed them when at play, teased the cat, and managed to get into everybody's way, but never volunteered to help any one. Yet Tom had a better nature, which needed awakening. Up to this time he did not obey his parents and endeavor to behave well, nor feel that he had a Father in heaven who loved and cared for him, and who had given His Son to die on the cross to save him from sin. Had he realized this, surely he would not have said to his sister Sally, "No one gives me credit for being good, so I may as well be naughty."

The proposed holiday was to be spent in catching crabs. Tom started off by appointment to meet his friend directly after his father had gone to the quarries.

"We shall have a first-rate day," called out Dick, who was awaiting his arrival; "but we should do a deal better if we had the little boat that Harry keeps for running across to Dixtown with. Isn't he gone fishing with Will? I thought I saw them start early last evening, and I haven't noticed them come back again."

"They ain't back again; but for all that, I can't take the boat," answered Tom. "If Harry comes soon he's very likely to go over to Dixtown, and if his boat ain't there, and he finds out I've taken it, he'll thrash me; for he won't care to row the big boat over, it's so much harder to pull."

"O, do take it!" urged Dick. "I'm going for a holiday to please you, and now you won't do the very thing that'll make our outing more jolly. I'll be off to the quarries if you're going to be so ill-natured."

"But I don't want Harry to thrash me; I know he will if he finds his boat gone."

"He won't want the boat to-day; he's sure to go to bed directly he lands, for he's been up all night."

"But suppose he's got fish to sell, he must go to Dixtown at once."

"Most likely they'll call at Dixtown on their way home and leave the fish."

"If I were only sure of that, I'd fetch the boat," said Tom, showing signs of yielding to Dick's temptation.

"You know they hardly ever come home without calling at Dixtown by the way."

"But they do sometimes."

"I've never found you a coward before, Tom," sneered Dick, pretending to leave him. "Good-bye, you Molly."

"O, don't go!" called out Tom. "I'll take the boat if you'll come with me; for we shan't have a day together again for ever so long."

"That's just what I thought, and why I wanted you to make use of Harry's boat. We can go to the Lion's Cave; it's a jolly place for crabs. We shall never lose sight of Norton Island; so, after all, we shall be close at home."

"The Lion's Cave is too far," said Tom; "I couldn't get home before Harry if I saw his boat in the distance."

"Then stay where you are," retorted Dick; "I shan't ask you again. You're the biggest coward I ever saw in my life. You'd better go back home at once."

Tom winced under Dick's words, and was conquered by them. "I'm no coward," he said, hastily. "I'll prove it too. Come along!"

The boys stole quietly down the narrow pathway that led to the small landing stage.

"Take the anchor with you," said Dick, jumping into the boat. "We shall want it; for we can't land against the rocks in Lion's Cave unless we've got it; the boat would drift away."

"All right," answered Tom. "I only wish I'd brought something to eat; we shall be so hungry."

"I've a loaf tied up in my handkerchief," replied Dick; "it's a good big one, quite enough for us two. I begged it of mother, for I said we were going to catch crabs, and I shouldn't be home to dinner."

"I told Sally I was off for the day with you, but I never thought about being hungry," said Tom.

"Don't mind, we shall get on somehow. We can't starve with this."

"And we won't be very late home," added Tom.

Each boy took an oar, and pulled hard. They rounded Norton Island, then St. Helen's, which communicated with it at low water; from thence they kept close under the cliffs, passing

fantastic crags, abrupt precipices, and dark
caverns.

"There's the old Lion at last," cried Dick.
"It's taken us a good three hours to get here;
but hasn't it been a splendid row? Ain't you
glad you came in the boat?"

"Yes, it's been very nice," answered Tom;
"but I should have liked it a deal more if I'd
been sure Harry wouldn't find me out."

"Don't worry about Harry, but enjoy your
holiday, my boy," said Dick. "It's a splendid
place for crabs. We'll land here first, and go to
the other caves afterwards if we've time; it's
just about low water. Doesn't the old Lion look
splendid?"

"He looks ready to spring at us. You
wouldn't admire him quite so much if you
didn't know he was a stone," remarked Tom.

"Perhaps not," said Dick, springing out of the
boat. "Make haste, Tom, and throw the rope
round that tall boulder; we've two good hours
before the tide will hurt us."

Tom did as he was bid.

"That's right. Now let's go to work."

The boys searched the clefts of the rocks, and
turned over heavy stones, hoping to surprise
their victims. Dick took care only to poke his
stick into the holes, but he was always ready to
haul Tom up on his shoulders so that he mighty
thrust his hand in and catch the crabs by their

laws. They soon captured four, which they tied together; then they chased a large one in a pool. After some time they managed to force him on to a rock; but here he stretched out his claws, and seemed so inclined to fight for his liberty, that even Tom could not be persuaded to handle him. At last Dick turned him over on his back with his stick, and then he was easily secured.

The search for crabs was very enticing; the boys wandered far beyond the Lion's cave in their eagerness, and both the tide and the boat were forgotten. A great splashing of water reminded them at last that time was passing quickly, and they discovered that they had rounded a point against which the waves were breaking. "Here's a pretty go," said Dick; "we must scale the top of the rock."

"I don't believe we can," answered Tom; "we'd better paddle."

"Nonsense, it isn't possible; the sea is too strong, you couldn't stand in it. I'll go over first and give you a help up."

But in spite of Dick's help, poor Tom's knuckles were badly grazed, and to make matters worse, when he was nearly landed in a place of safety, he let go the string which held the crabs, for his companion as usual made him carry the spoil.

"You must go back for the crabs," shouted
Dick; "after all the trouble we've had in
catching them, I ain't going to see them thrown
away."

So Tom had to retrace his steps. When he
secured his prey, he found he could not drag
them and himself too on the ledge where his
friend stood; finally he threw the crabs up, and
Dick caught hold of the end of the string.

"Now we're up here, I don't see very well
how we shall get on," said Dick.

True enough, as Tom found when he looked
down the perpendicular slab, which must be
scaled before the cave was reached. The tide
was coming in so rapidly, there was no time to
waste.

"Be quick," called Dick; "I mean to let
myself down—you do the same; we shall fall
on the sand."

"I can't and won't carry the crabs," said Tom.
"If you want them, you may take them."

"You shall carry them," answered Dick,
angrily.

"I tell you I won't."

Dick saw that Tom was not to be awed by
any threats, so he answered more pleasantly,
"Don't be unkind; I'll bear my part. I'll slip
down first and you let the crabs down after me;
I'll catch them."

But he found the slab higher than he calculated; he did not fall on the sand, but on a rock, which bruised him considerably, and made him very cross. The crabs fell more comfortably, but poor Tom managed to tumble and hit his forehead on the edge of a sharp stone. He was stunned for a moment, the pain was so sharp.

"Come along," cried Dick, who had gone forward with the crabs. "Make haste, or you'll be washed away by the tide. Get past the next point, and there's the cave."

Tom followed his companion with a very bad grace.

"I've hurt my head," he said, when he and Dick were safe in the cave.

"It's nothing, only a scratch. What a fuss you made about a trifle! We've no time to lose; we must paddle to the boat. Pull off your boots."

"I wish I'd never come," said Tom, whose eye was smarting, and made worse by rubbing it with his hand, which was wet with salt water.

"It's too late to be sorry now," laughed Dick. "Be quick, or Harry will be home before you."

These words had more effect than any he could have chosen. Tom did not linger again, but pulled well with his oar all the way to Norton Island.

When they passed St. Helen's he looked out anxiously for his brothers. But he escaped a thrashing; for they were so successful, they put into Dixtown to sell their fish, and did not arrive home until an hour after the boys.

"We've had a famous day," said Dick, when they had anchored he boat. "Now let's divide the crabs. I'm to have the biggest, because I carried them."

"I had them longest."

Dick did not contest the point, but, as usual, managed to appropriate the best to himself.

"I'll see you to-morrow," he said to Tom at parting. "Your eye only wants bathing; it will be all right by the morning."

Tom was very much inclined to slink in at the back, to avoid meeting his parents. But he was very hungry: so taking up his crabs, he went boldly up to the front door.

"Bless me, Tom!" cried his mother, as he entered, "what an eye you've got! Look, father!" she added, speaking to her husband. "What will Miss Pringle think of him?'

"It's nothing to me what sort of an eye he's got," answered Mr. Gillies. "He's been with Dick Potter all day, and up to mischief again. He shall go to his situation to-morrow however bad he may be."

"Go and bathe it directly," said his mother. "Sally, fetch some warm water."

"Come, Tom, there's a good boy!" called his sister. "Let's go into the kitchen. What splendid crabs you've got. We'll boil one or two of the smallest for supper, and Harry will sell the best tomorrow."

Tom was soon sitting by the fire giving Sally an account of the day's proceedings, but he did not tell her how far he and Dick had been, nor that he had taken his brother's boat at his friend's suggestion.

CHAPTER V.

HOW TOM SPENT HIS LAST DAY AT HOME.

WHEN Tom awoke, he could scarcely open his eye, it was so stiff and sore. No one pitied him, and he knew very well he deserved no sympathy, and that, if the truth were known, he would be severely punished. One wrong step led to another, and before breakfast was over he had told several untruths to hide his fault. First he said he had walked across the low ridge of rocks which united St. Helen's to Norton Island, and had a heavy fall; then, when one of his brothers asked if Dick were with him, he answered, "Only a part of the time."

He felt very uncomfortable when Sally put his question, "Was your little boat at home yesterday, Harry? I went down to look if you were coming, and I didn't see it at the landing stage."

"But I did," answered Tom, hastily, putting his hand up to his eye, as if it pained him, but really to hide his confusion. "It was there when I went to St. Helen's."

"Perhaps I overlooked it," said Sally; and the conversation ended at this point; for Harry seemingly did not notice the question.

Tom was thankful to escape detection, and he felt no compunction at having volunteered so many falsehoods.

"Stay at home to-day, and see if you can't get that eye of yours better, Tom," said his father, as he left the room to go to his work. "It makes you look as if you'd been fighting. Mind, no excuses to-morrow—nothing must hinder you from going with your mother, the first thing in the morning, to Miss Pringle."

"Your clothes will be all ready," remarked Mrs. Gillies. "You've a change of shirts, and a good second-hand suit for Sunday. The every-day one you've got now will serve for some months yet. Never was a boy better started off. I wish you'd be a bit thankful."

"You don't expect me to be, so I don't disappoint you," answered Tom, carelessly.

"Was there ever such a boy!" said his mother, angrily. "It's a good thing you stand alone in the family. Do for once be obedient, and keep indoors quietly to-day. I'm going to Dixtown. Now, I tell you what I'll do, Tom," she added more kindly. "If you stay and bathe your eye,

I'll sell your crabs, and buy you a pair of boots with the money they fetch."

"All right, mother!" he replied, going into the kitchen. "Come, Sally, give me plenty of hot water."

Tom was very quiet for the first hour, then he grew tired of doing nothing, so he strolled out for a little walk, hoping he should meet Dick. But as the latter had a day's work at the quarries, there was no chance of that. At last he sat down at the edge of the cliff overlooking the landing stage, and amused himself, as usual, by throwing stones about in all directions. He stopped when he saw a very handsome tabby cat creeping slowly along; she belonged to his grandmother, old Mrs. Gillies, who lived in a small cottage on the island. Tom disliked his grandmother, and knew that the cat heralded her approach. He was right; grandmother followed close behind her favorite. When she came near to her grandson, she asked, "How did you get that black eye, Tom?"

"What does it matter to you, grandmother?" answered the boy rudely; "but if you want very much to know, I fell on the low rocks over against St. Helen's."

"You didn't, Tom. You were doing what you'd no right to do. I saw you in Harry's boat yesterday. Did he lend it to you?"

"That's no business of yours," retorted Tom, angrily.

"But it is my business, and I mean to know the truth. I shall ask Harry if he lent his boat to you."

"So you may, grandmother, and he'll say yes."

"You've told a story, you hardened boy. How glad I am you're going away from here! I mean to call at your father's this evening. Harry shall know that you took his boat; you deserve a good whipping. You didn't go to the low rocks. I saw you and Dick Potter start in the boat, and I watched your return. I might perhaps have kept your secret if you hadn't been so pert this morning. I am going over to Dixtown until evening; but expect to see me on my return."

Tom had no time to answer, for Mrs. Gillies made her way quickly down the pathway to the landing stage where an old fisherman and his wife were awaiting her arrival.

Grandmother's cottage was her own, and she had a pension of four shillings a week, which just sufficed to keep her, with the help of sea-bird's eggs, crabs, mussels, and such like food. It was strange that she should prefer going to Dixtown with her neighbors, rather than her relations. This arose out of her independence; she did not care to be under any obligation to her own kindred; for though she admired her son greatly, her grandchildren did not inspire much love, and she really disliked Tom.

The cat waited until the boat which contained her mistress was fairly off, then she came slowly up the sloping pathway.

Tom watched her, and as he watched, a wicked, mischievous, thought entered his head. "I'll be thrashed for something," he said aloud. "Miss Tabby shall catch it, and grandmother will find that if she tells of me she'll be paid back again."

Thus speaking, he seized an old tin saucepan which had been thrown out of one of the cottages, and had lain for many a day among the rocks. "Tabby, Tabby!" he called, and then looked round to see if any one were near. No one was in sight, so he called again, "Tabby, Tabby!"

As a rule the cat avoided Tom; but perhaps his voice sounded more gentle than usual, and poor Tabby felt lonely without her mistress. Be that as it may, she came and rubbed her nose against him.

Tom felt in his pocket for string. Unfortunately he found enough for his purpose. He stroked and petted the cat, and meanwhile made one end of the string fast to the old saucepan, which had lost its handle, but had a great hole in the side that served Tom's purpose just as well. The next thing to be done was to tie the other end to pussy's tail, and this was rather a more difficult matter, but was managed at last by means of a slip-knot.

When all was arranged, Tom carried Tabby a little way down the pathway, and then let her run. So as soon as the poor creature heard the noise behind her, she flew along to escape it. Round and round she went, and up and down; but the same noise followed her. At last she bounded down the cliff, far our of Tom's sight. He pursued her, and was in time to see her flying backwards and forwards over the rocks. He called her, but she was too wild with fear to heed his voice, and ere he was near enough to catch her, she plunged headlong into the sea, which was rather stormy, and was quickly carried out by the tide.

Tom threw off his socks and boots, and paddled out so far as he dare, but he was too late to do any good. Tabby and her saucepan were far away, and the last he saw of the one friend his grandmother prized in the world was pussy floating on the waves.

Tom was aghast at his work. He would willingly have endured a thrashing could he have brought the poor cat back again to life. He watched the waves until he lost sight of her, and then he walked slowly away. No one had seen him, but even that comfort did not avail; for he knew that he had acted a dastardly part.

He was conscience-stricken; the mentor within told him he was a cruel, inhuman boy. He went directly home, and sat at the cottage door for the rest of the day. He was not afraid of his grandmother suspecting him until after he had left home, for the cat sometimes absented herself for hours together; but what if Pussy and the saucepan should be washed on the shore when the tide turned?— that would tell tales of some one.

Mrs. Gillies reached home towards afternoon, and busied herself in arranging Tom's clothes. She had bought him a strong pair of boots, and several other articles of dress, at Dixtown.

"I was determined to give you a good start, Tom," she said. "I couldn't have a son of mine go to his first place without proper things, so I added a little money to the couple of shillings the crabs fetched."

"Thank you, mother," answered Tom, but in such a subdued voice, Mrs. Gillies thought he was awed at the prospect of leaving home.

"Cheer up, lad," she said kindly. "Only be a good boy, and you'll please your father and me, and we shan't find fault with you any more."

Tom burst into tears at these words which astonished his mother still more; so, by way of changing the conversation, she added, "Have you said good-bye to your grandmother?"

"I saw her this morning for a minute," replied Tom, drying his eyes quickly. "She's gone to Dixtown for the day."

"What a stormy passage she'll have home! She oughtn't to go like this without consulting the boys. But I suppose she will have her own way."

Every footfall that passed, Tom thought that grandmother was coming, and when the evening closed without seeing her, the boy felt even more repentant, for perhaps, after all, she was better disposed towards him than she had seemed to be in the morning. He had a miserable night, for he dreamed of Tabby and the saucepan and granny's anger from the time he fell asleep until he awoke in the morning.

His brothers were so kind to him before he left, that he was sorely inclined to tell Harry how badly he had behaved, and he would have done so in all probability, had not the latter gone off early, leaving Will to row him and his mother over to Dixtown.

"Good-bye, Tom," said his father, shaking hands with him. "You must never expect to come home again for good. Remember this is the turning-point in your life; and if you don't stay with Miss Pringle, you must find another situation, or starve, for I can't keep idle fellows here."

Tom looked anxiously in the direction of his grandmother's cottage as he went to the boat, but all seemed quiet as usual. "She may never find me out," he thought; "and if she does, I shall be far enough away to escape a punishment."

Still the boy was unhappy. Another reason which made him rather out of spirits was not having seen Dick Potter on the previous day. It so happened Dick was home very late, and went to bed directly, nor did he feel inclined to get up earlier than he was obliged, in order to say "good-bye" to his friend.

His comments to himself, as he worked at the quarries, might have been summed up in these words: "Tom'll miss *me*, but he'll be just as useful to me at Dixtown as here; in fact more useful, for I shall have a day with him in the town when it suits me."

CHAPTER VI.

TOM AT HIS SITUATION.

THE boat reached the landing stage by seven o'clock on Saturday morning.

"Carry your bundle, Tom, and follow me," said his mother. "I'll just take you to Miss Pringle, and then I'm off to sell my prawns."

As Mrs. Gillies passed up the narrow street where Mother Crampton lived, she stopped for a moment to speak to the dame, who was standing at her door.

"Good morning, mother," she said. "This is my son. He's the one I told you was going to live with Miss Pringle."

The old woman smiled kindly at Tom. She liked the expression of his face. "How different she is to Grandmother Gillies!" thought the boy; "I'm sure I shouldn't tease her cat."

"Is your name Tom?" she asked.

"Yes," answered Mrs. Gillies. "He was christened Thomas, but we generally call him Tom, sometimes Tommy, it doesn't matter which. He's on his own account from this day. I'm sure he's old enough to earn his living."

"I hope I shall hear that you're doing well," said Mother Crampton, looking at Tom. "You may call and see me whenever you've half an hour to spare."

"Thank you!" he answered.

"That's kind of you; for he won't be able to come home very often on Saturday, because of his having to be back on Sunday evening to be ready for Monday morning's baking," added Mrs. Gillies. "Our being on that bit of an island makes us obliged to fetch him and send him back. There isn't a fisherman in Dixtown who'd do the journey one way under a shilling."

"Couldn't either of your sons help him?" asked Mother Crampton.

"They'll help him when business calls them here, but they work so hard, poor fellows, I couldn't ask them to come on purpose."

"Then, Tom, I'll invite you to spend any Sunday evening that Miss Pringle spares you with me; but remember, I'm a quiet old body, and can't bear noise. Will you like to come?" asked Mother Crampton.

"O, yes, please," answered the boy; "and I'm sure I could sit still if you'd talk to me."

Mrs. Gillies looked surprised. "He's behaving like a gentleman, I declare," she said.

"He's subdued like, because he's got a black eye. He went out and fell over the rocks. But come, Tom; I haven't any more time to spend in gossip."

Tom allowed his mother to go forward a few steps, and then he turned to Dame Crampton and said, "I don't believe I shall ever want to be mischievous when I'm with you. Good-bye!"

The mother and son walked briskly through the town, and soon reached the baker's shop which was to be Tom's home. Miss Pringle had just finished her breakfast in the kitchen. She had prepared a second bowl of porridge for her new boy, for she expected him to arrive early, and felt she could not very well suffer him to be hungry until dinner time; and, in fact, there was no economy in so doing, for he would only eat more then. She came into the shop when she heard the sound of voices, and Tom met his mistress for the first time.

After a few preliminaries were arranged, and Miss Pringle had asked Tom how he came by his black eye, his mother said, "I shall call for his clothes every Saturday. Of course, I shall wash and mend them for him, and I dare say I shall look in now and then to see how he's getting on."

"I never encourage much intercourse with home, Mrs. Gillies," answered Miss Pringle, stiffly. "I keep my boy fully occupied, and always find he works better if he doesn't see too much of his relations."

"O! Very well; it's the same to me. I'll only come and fetch the clothes on Saturday;" and nodding to her son, Mrs. Gillies left the shop and walked up the street crying, "Who'll buy fine prawns?"

She was so fortunate in finding customers that she was ready to return home at noon; but knowing that Will would be busy in Dixtown until one o'clock, she went to Mother Crampton's to spend the spare hour.

We must return to Tom.

"Follow me," said Miss Pringle as soon as they were alone. Tom took up his parcel and walked behind his new mistress into the kitchen. He stood at the window and watched her while she went to the fire and set on a saucepan. In a few moments he heard her say, "It's nice and hot now," and then she poured the contents into a basin of exactly the same dimensions as one already standing on a round table.

She placed the basin, with an iron spoon, opposite to her own and sat down, and pointing to a wooden stool, ordered Tom to take his place. He did so, and found himself face to face with Miss Pringle, who was unlike any one he had ever seen before. He wondered how he

should ever get on with her, for he already felt
quite subdued in her presence.

"Your name is Thomas, I think," she said, in
a grave voice.

"Yes, missus, but I'm most always called
Tom."

"Say, 'Yes, Miss Pringle.' I always like my
name pronounced by my boys when they
address me. Now hear what I have to say.
Don't think I'm a rich woman, Tom; I'm very
poor, and have hard work to earn my living;
therefore, I expect my boy to do his best to
save me from all unnecessary expense. As to
your food, you live just the same as I do, so
there can't be any grumbling about not being
well fed. Would you like me to tell you exactly
what you have to do all day?"

"Yes, Miss Pringle."

"We rise at five o'clock in summer, six in
winter, and on Sundays at seven all the year
round. You will hear the clock strike, and know
when to get up. I expect you to be dressed and
waiting for me in the kitchen by a quarter past
five; but I do not wish you to unfasten a shutter
or undraw a bolt until I come down stairs.
When we have opened the house you will have
to heat the oven while I make the bread; then
you will sweep out the shop and dust the
bottles of sweets that stand in the window.
Mind, I don't allow you to take a single drop; I

shall prosecute you if you touch one; it's the kindest thing for me to do, and will save you, perhaps, from being hanged; for great crimes generally come out of little beginnings.

"You have to scrub the shop floor once a week, but you must wash the stone steps every morning. Then you have to carry the bread out, attend to the garden, fetch water, gather the fruit and sell it, and do just whatever is wanted. I'm quite as particular about the fruit as the sweets; if I find you eating a bruised apple I shall stop off part of your dinner; but if you gather an apple or a peach, I shall give you into the policeman's hands.

"I've forgotten one thing here in the house, that is the stairs; you have to sweep them down every morning. My bedroom is always locked, for I attend to that myself; and the gentleman and his daughter who lodge with me want nothing from you except civility. Now and then I shall not mind your going home on Saturday until Sunday evening, but only as a great treat; for, as I told your mother, I don't encourage too much visiting of any kind. You'll go to church with me on Sunday morning, and after dinner your time is your own until half-past seven in winter, and half-past eight in summer."

While Miss Pringle was speaking, Tom played with his iron spoon, for he did not like to begin to eat without receiving her permission. She now signified to him that he should take his porridge, and she handed him a thick slice of stale read.

"It's very good bread, and not too new," she said. "I often wonder how my customers can do with it so fresh from the oven; it's very bad for their digestion."

Tom soon dispatched his porridge, but he found it a harder matter to eat the bread, so he quietly slipped what remained of his slice into his pocket, when his mistress was making up the kitchen fire.

"Now you've finished, I'll show you where you sleep, and a drawer in which you may keep your clothes," said Miss Pringle.

"Bring your bundle with you. This is your room," and she pointed to the hole under the staircase. "You have a comfortable bed here, and I allow you clean sheets once a month. This top drawer," and she opened one of a chest that stood in a recess between the kitchen and staircase, "is for your clothes. You can wash in the kitchen; I allow you a clean towel once a fortnight. I will show you where you may keep it; and you will always find soap in the dish by the side of the sink. Unpack your clothes, and then come to me in the kitchen."

Tom was too much surprised to speak. He had been accustomed to rough food and a hard bed, but he had never eaten such stale bread before, nor slept in a blackhole under the staircase.

He soon disposed of his small wardrobe in the one drawer allotted to him, and then went to Miss Pringle, who was sweeping the shop. "This is scrubbing day," she called out when she saw him enter. "Take the pail to the pump, and fill it with fresh water, and let me see you go to work."

Tom filled the pail, and began to scrub for the first time in his life. He found it more difficult than he anticipated, for he had a hard mistress to please. First he held the brush wrongly; then he made the floor too wet; then he wasted the soap by leaving it in the water; and at last he could have cried with mortification.

Miss Pringle watched him for some time before she began to dust the bottles in the window. "These are the sweets, Tom, I spoke if," she said, tapping one of them with her knuckles. "Again I tell you that if you steal a single drop, you will find your way to the police-station."

Tom was a long time before he finished scrubbing the shop. Afterwards he was ordered to sweep the stairs. "They're only scrubbed once a month," said his mistress.

The boy found this task as difficult as the scrubbing, for he could not manage his great broom. He was laboring over the undertaking,

when a door at the top of the staircase opened, and a young girl appeared with a teapot. It was Annie Newton, who remembering what Mother Crampton had said about Tom, and seeing him, broom in hand, moved down the stairs to give her room to pass, said, "How do you do? I hope we shall soon be good friends."

Tom's heart warmed towards Annie; she looked so pleasant, and spoke to him as if he were her equal. So he answered, "Thank you, miss. Can I fill your teapot? The water doesn't quite boil, I know; I'll bring it up when it's ready."

Miss Pringle came out of the kitchen at this moment to look after Tom, so Annie thought it was better to fill the teapot herself.

"O, it's you, Miss Annie. Come for your hot water, I suppose," said the spinster. "That's my new boy; he isn't very handy yet, but I hope he'll turn out well when he's been properly taught. How's your father this morning?"

"Tolerably well, thank you," replied the young girl. "He seems in much better spirits about his eyesight."

Having filled her teapot, Annie passed Tom again, and smiled at him, as he stepped on one side to make way for her.

"I'll do anything for you," thought the boy. "How odd is it that, since I've been at Dixtown, I've seen two people that I don't think I could have behaved so badly to as I did to grandmother! I don't believe I should have taken Harry's boat if they'd been with me instead of Dick." And then Tom remembered the poor cat and its untimely end, and was so absorbed that he stood with his chin on the broom, and did not hear Miss Pringle come softly out of the kitchen to see what he was doing. She brought him back to himself by laying her hand heavily on his shoulder, and saying, "This won't do. I can't have an idle boy."

Tom looked very red, and set to work again, nor did he allow his attention to flag until he had finished Saturday's cleaning.

"What am I to do next?" he asked, appealing to his mistress.

"Carry out the bread," she replied. "That is the basket on the shelf. There are four families I send to. The people at the great house, they have six loaves. Then there is Mrs. Richards in High Street has three loaves; Mr. Johnson the butcher has three, and Mr. Smart the grocer three. Now mind, I allow no playing on the road; you must not be gone more than half an hour."

Tom walked away at a quick pace, and soon deposited his six loaves at the great house. "I won't be behind to-day," he muttered as he bent his steps toward the High Street. But Tom, it must be remembered, made resolutions in his own strength, and was infirm of purpose. He had not gone very far before he stopped to look at some boys playing marbles; and then at a sailor who was carrying home a toy sailing-boat, so that, though he hurried the rest of the way, he lost five minutes, which he could not make up.

Miss Pringle did not comment on his length of absence, and Tom hoped he had escaped reproof; but when dinner time came, he was informed that he would have dry bread and water, and no bacon, which Miss Pringle ate alone. She generally punished her boys for minor offences by stopping off part of their food, because it answered a two-fold purpose; saved her provisions, and taught them that they could not disobey her commands without reaping bitter consequences.

The boy felt very indignant. He would have promised to do better had she given him a kind word of remonstrance, but to be deprived of half his dinner made him rebellious.

"Take the basket and fill it with fallen apples," said his mistress later in the day.

Tom was no longer bright and happy, or inclined to be obedient. "The disagreeable old thing!" he murmured, as he walked down the garden. "I'll eat some, that I will."

He picked up the apples, which were scattered about in every direction, and ate as fast as he could meanwhile.

Opposite the apple-tree was a well-filled peach-tree. "How good they look! I'm sure she hasn't behaved so well at starting that I need be careful about taking just one," thought Tom. So he made a long step across the border and gathered the largest he could see. He put it hastily into his pocket, and was about to demolish it behind a shrub, when he heard his mistress call "Tom."

"She's seen me from the window," he exclaimed. "No, she's not," he added, for Miss Pringle was talking to a lady.

It was Mrs. Wyvil from the great house, who came to buy fruit. She looked into Tom's basket, and offered Miss Pringle two shillings for its contents. The offer was accepted, and Tom was ordered to carry them across at once; which he did after secreting the peach in his drawer as he passed the staircase.

The remainder of the day was spent in digging up potatoes and weeding the gravel walk. Tom was glad to pause for a quarter of an hour and sit down to his tea in the kitchen when the clock chimed the quarter. "At ten minutes to eight you may put away your tools and come to supper."

When the evening meal was concluded, Miss Pringle said, "I want you to read a chapter out of the Bible to me, Tom; but before you begin, tell me, on your honor, did you eat any apples?"

"No, Miss Pringle."

"I believe you. Now read the twentieth chapter of the book of Exodus."

Tom felt a twinge. After all, Miss Pringle was better than he believed her to be; for she supposed that he told the truth. He had a second twinge when he read the commandments through, for had he not stolen? Was not the peach in a corner of his drawer?

"I allow you ten minutes to get into bed, Tom," said his mistress. "Don't be longer."

The boy took care to put the peach under his pillow, lest Miss Pringle should look into his drawer when she came to take away his candle. So soon as he was alone he ate it, but he did not enjoy it in the least, for he could not forget the words he had been reading. "Thou shalt not steal," came to him again and again; and, somehow, the peach and grandmother's cat were strangely mixed up in his dreams; so, though he slept soundly, he felt very tired and miserable when he awoke next morning.

CHAPTER VII.

THE DEAD CAT.

GRANDMOTHER GILLIES did not carry out her intention of calling on her son to complain of Tom, because she was so late home from Dixtown. She made up her mind she never would trust to her neighbors again, for she had to sit on the harbor wall for two hours, waiting until the fisherman and his wife were ready to return. She had appointed to meet them at a given time, and they had failed to keep the appointment. She was afraid to leave her post lest they should come in her absence, and yet she wanted a cup of tea to warm her so much; for though it was August, there was a brisk wind, and Grandmother Gillies did not bear the chilly evening air at seventy as she had done at twenty years old.

The trio did not leave the harbor until after sunset, and when they were half way to Norton Island it blew such a gale that the boat advanced very slowly, for the fisherman was an old man, and unable to pull the oars so vigorously as Harry or Will Gillies.

Grandmother was thankful to reach home. She found her cottage window half open, as she had left it, to admit Tabby, if the cat chose to take shelter there in her absence. She busied herself in making a fire and boiling her kettle of water; and when she had disposed of a large cup of tea and a good slice of bread and butter, she felt better, and the world smiled on her again.

"I wonder where Tabby is?" she said aloud; for she had a habit of talking to herself. "I mustn't let her go without her milk. Tabby, Tabby!" she called from the window.

As the cat did not appear, grandmother set aside the saucer of milk, and, having washed up her tea things, and put them back into the cupboard, settled into her armchair by the fire.

"I'm just tired out," she muttered. "I've had a good warning not to trust other people again. Harry and Will know how to pull, and wouldn't keep me waiting for a couple of hours."

Before grandmother retired to her bedroom she went to the window and opened it just wide enough for Tabby to squeeze through if she came later, and then she discovered that large drops of rain were falling.

"Why, it's just beginning to rain!" she exclaimed. "Tabby hates rain; she'll be sure to come now. I'll wait another ten minutes and close the window, for the wet beats in. Tabby will take good care to knock, and I shall hear her." So grandmother again took refuge in her arm-chair, and this time she fell fast asleep.

When she awoke, the fire was out and the clock struck eleven. She roused herself up and found the lucifers to light a candle; she then opened the window, expecting to find Tabby without, and very cross at being unable to get in. She was a little surprised that the cat was not there, but no thought of an accident having happened to her favorite crossed her mind. "She'll be here before morning. I'll leave the window as I generally do when she's out," said the old woman.

Grandmother Gillies was up betimes, and her first thought was of Tabby. When she discovered no trace of her, she began to wonder where she was.

"I certainly saw her close to the landing stage when the boat started. Ah! And Tom was there too; but he wouldn't touch her, I know."

She was still debating in her own mind as to Tabby's whereabouts, when the door was opened, and her granddaughter Sally entered.

"Good morning, granny," she said. "I came to see how you were after the storm. Mother has taken Tom over to Dixtown, and she couldn't come herself. She was afraid you'd have a tossing yesterday."

"So I did, Sally. Was Tom's eye better?"

"O, yes; much better, granny. But how are you?"

"What did Tom do yesterday? I saw him on the cliffs opposite the landing stage when I started," asked the old woman without heeding Sally's question.

"He said he saw you. He was at home nigh upon all day. He didn't seem in good spirits."

Grandmother was relieved. She did not really imagine that Tom would injure her cat, and yet she was glad to know that he was at home for the greater part of the day, and never suspected that he had accomplished his cruel work so immediately after she left him.

"How are you, granny?" asked Sally again. "You don't seem quite yourself. Mother was afraid the storm would upset you."

"No, it hasn't, child; but the fact is Tabby's never been home all night, and I'm a little uneasy about her."

"But she often serves you so."

"Not if it rains; she never stays out in the wet."

"I dare say she won't be long. She'll be wanting her breakfast. Shall I walk round the island and see if I can find any trace of her?"

"Do, there's a good girl; and come back to me before you go home."

Sally went off at once, asking the few people she met by the way if they had seen the cat, for Tabby was just as well known as any other inhabitant of the island. She was on the point of returning to her grandmother, to inform her that her errand had been a fruitless one, when she thought she would go down to the shore. The tide was running out fast, and Tabby might be in one of the caves catching small crabs.

It did not take her many minutes to reach the landing stage; she walked along the sands, peering into every corner, and calling "Tabby! Tabby!" As she was passing a small nook, where several high stones were firmly fixed in the sand, and covered with thick brown sea-weed, something darker than the weed attracted her attention.

Sally walked up to it to gratify her curiosity, and not because she expected to find Tabby; and then she discovered it was the body of the once petted cat, which had evidently been preyed upon by some creature, for she had a large hole in her side, and half her tail was gone. As Sally gazed in wonderment and horror, a great crab sidled away, as if it had been disturbed, and sought to hide from detection. It was quite evident that poor pussy had fallen a victim to its voracious propensities, but how she came to be reduced to such a condition as to afford food for a crab was more than the young girl could tell.

"What will grandmother say? Who will carry the poor cat home to her? I dare not," she exclaimed. "Oh! What shall I do?"

She sat down near the dead creature, but shrank from touching her, and kept repeating to herself, in a monotonous voice, "What will grandmother say?"

She was aroused by a sound of whistling. It was Dick Potter, who was on his way to the quarries.

"O, Dick! Do come here," called Sally. "Tabby's dead; it's so dreadful."

The boy scrambled, and jumped, and slid, until he reached her side. "What's up?" he asked.

"Look! Look!" cried Sally, pointing with her finger.

"It's a dead cat, that's all. It ain't a very uncommon thing to find one, and I suppose the crabs have been at it."

"But it's Tabby," almost screamed Sally, "grandmother's cat; and I can't touch her, she looks so horrible. I don't know what granny will say when she sees her. She'll be quite ill."

"I'll carry it up to the old woman if you like, but you must go on first and say I'm coming."

"I'd rather you went with me to help tell her."

"Nonsense! What's a cat?" said Dick, scornfully.

"A great deal to grandmother," answered Sally indignantly. "But I'll be obliged to you if you'll carry Tabby home," she added more gently.

Dick touched the cat with a short stick he carried and finally held her by the small bit that yet remained of her once beautiful tail.

Grandmother stood at her open door watching for Sally to come. She did not notice that Dick was behind her granddaughter and asked, "Have you found her?"

"Yes, grandmother," replied Sally, hesitating.

"Where is she?" said the old woman, walking forward a few steps; and then she caught sight of Dick carrying her dead Tabby.

"You wicked, wicked boy!" she screamed. "How dare you kill my cat? I'll have you punished."

"A nice way to thank a fellow!" exclaimed Dick, throwing down his burden. "You may bury her yourself; I won't help you." And he was turning away, but Sally called out—

"It wasn't Dick, grandmother; Tabby's fallen over the cliffs into the sea. I found her on the shore, and the crabs have had her."

"Tabby fallen, indeed! She was too sure-footed for that. O, my poor, poor cat!" and grandmother burst into tears.

Bad and hardened as Dick was, he felt a momentary sorrow for old Mrs. Gillies. "I ain't worth much," he said, "but I wouldn't kill your Tabby for fun."

"You must believe him," cried Sally; "depend on it I'm right. Tabby fell over the cliffs."

"I wish I hadn't gone out yesterday; every thing went wrong," sobbed poor granny. "I suppose Tabby must have tumbled. I'd have locked her up if I'd have thought she would have got into mischief. She always has walked on the most dangerous places. O, dear! I don't know how I shall get on without her."

Sally tried to comfort the old woman, but Dick's sympathy was soon exhausted. "I'm off to work now," he said.

"I thought you'd help bury her, and now you're going away. Won't you stay and dig a hole?" asked grandmother.

"If you've done making a fuss, and are ready for business, I'll stay," answered Dick rudely. "Where's a spade?"

"I'll get one," replied Sally.

"I can't bear to part with her," sighed grandmother, stroking the mangled remains of her poor favorite, while Dick was busy digging.

"We must find another kitten for you," answered Sally, kindly; "there are plenty of kittens to be had for asking."

"But none will ever be so faithful as my poor dear Tabby."

The grave was made in the small garden behind the cottage. Grandmother watched Dick until he had finished, and a little mound was raised over Tabby's remains.

"Here's twopence for you," she said, "and thank you."

Dick was not generous enough to refuse payment; he put the coppers into his pocket, and went away to find work.

"You can go home now, Sally," said grandmother; "I'd rather be alone."

It was a long day for the old woman, who shed many tears over poor Tabby's untimely end. Could Tom have witnessed her grief, he would have been doubly punished.

Mr. Gillies and his son Harry called in the evening, and heard the sad history a second time; for Sally had already told them every particular.

"I shall soon find you a new pet, granny," said Harry, when he bade her good-bye. "Don't fret."

"I'd rather not have another just yet," she replied.

"You'd best leave your grandmother to herself," remarked Mr. Gillies to his son, as they walked home. "It's no use trying to mend matters while the trouble's so fresh. She's better without a cat for a time."

"I shall ornament Tabby's grave tomorrow," was grandmother's last thought ere she fell asleep. And here we may as well add, that before many days passed, the little mound was studded with whelks and oyster shells and in the center a fuchsia was planted which cost a shilling; but granny did not grudge the money, nor the sacrifice it entailed to purchase it.

CHAPTER VIII.

SUNDAY WITH MISS PRINGLE.

TOM thought seven o'clock never would come on Sunday morning. He was up and dressed soon after five, but he dare not open the house, having received orders to wait in the kitchen.

Miss Pringle was down stairs punctually, and after wishing Tom good morning, told him to unfasten the shutters and unbolt the doors. This was soon done. Then he received instructions to carry a pail to the well in the garden, and fill it with water.

"I'm very lucky," said his mistress. "While all the people in Dixtown are short of water and have to go to the public spring, my well is supplied."

This announcement did not particularly interest Tom, moreover he was impatient to get into the garden. "I don't believe I can stay here long," he muttered, as he walked along swinging his pail. "I must have fresh air, and here's a little to be got in my present quarters."

Tom had a sensation of enjoyment he had never experienced before as he looked at the flowers and felt the warm sunlight. "How beautiful Norton Island will be today; how I shall like to peep at it this afternoon!" he thought; and then he sighed, and said aloud, "I've been silly, very silly, not to find steady work nearer home. I declare I shall miss them all. I wonder if I really am much worse than other boys?"

"Make haste, Tom," called out Miss Pringle, in a sharp, shrill voice.

The boy began to pump, and the water came at first, slowly; but before his pail was full it ceased altogether.

Tom pumped on for some minutes, but not another drop could he get. "It's no use trying any more," he said. "I must just go and tell her what's happened."

On his way back he picked up an apple that lay in his path, and began eating it.

"What did you throw away just now?" asked his mistress, coming out to meet him.

"A bit of an apple, Miss Pringle," said Tom.

"How dare you touch my fruit?"

"It was a very bad one, and only fit for the pigs, Miss Pringle."

"Bad or not bad, you shall obey me. I shall punish you for it. Why have you not filled the pail?"

"There isn't any more water in the well," answered Tom, rudely.

"I don't' believe it. You haven't pumped properly."

"But I know I have. You'd better go and try the pump yourself."

"Speak respectfully, Tom. After you have filled the kettle, follow me, for I intend you to pump while I look on."

Tom did as he was told, but not pleasantly. As they passed the peach-trees Miss Pringle stopped to count her peaches.

"One gone," she said angrily. "You've taken it, Tom."

"Suppose I haven't, Miss Pringle."

"Did you, or did you not take it, sir?"

"No, Miss Pringle," replied Tom positively, and moved toward the pump.

"I wish I'd never taken him; he seems worse than other boys, and more difficult to manage," thought the spinster. "Now, Tom, pump," she said aloud.

The boy pumped again, but with the same result; and at length his mistress was obliged to confess, though very reluctantly, that she must do as others had done for some weeks, make use of the public spring.

"It's most provoking, Tom," she said; "you must be very careful of the water we've got, for I don't intend you to fetch any to-day. I'm not going to have the neighbors giggling at my expense on Sunday. You can only wash your hands once more to-day, and Miss Newton must do with a short allowance. Now come to breakfast."

Miss Pringle had prepared the porridge when Annie came into the kitchen. She wished Tom and her landlady good morning, and made some remark about the fine day.

"I'm in great trouble," whined Miss Pringle, without returning her greeting.

"What is the matter?"

"My pump has gone dry, Miss Annie."

"But with such a beautiful spring so near, that need not trouble you," answered the young girl, cheerfully.

"You're just like all other children, Miss Newton; as if any public spring could be as good as a private well. You will find out I'm right before the day is out, for you must do with what water you have up stairs for washing. I've only just enough for the teapots."

"I'm afraid I cannot do without a small jugful in addition; papa needs some warm water to bathe his eyes with."

"He can't have any, Miss Annie. Tomorrow there will be plenty."

"You can beg a little from next door, Miss Pringle. Mrs. Wilkins fills her large tub every Saturday for Sunday's use."

"I'm surprised at you, miss. Do you think I mean to sink so low as to ask my neighbor to give me water?"

"There is nothing to be ashamed of," answered Annie, with some spirit; "but at any rate, if you dislike asking Mrs. Wilkins, I can do so; poor papa cannot go without warm water for his eyes."

"May I fetch you a jugful from the spring?" asked Tom, eagerly.

"Thomas, you forget yourself," said Miss Pringle, angrily. "It is not my habit to send my boy out to fetch water on Sunday."

"Thank you all the same for your kind offer, Tom," replied Annie; "I shall manage somehow," she added, as she left the kitchen. She was half way up the stairs when the thought occurred to her that he might be without books, so she returned once more, and said, "If you come up stairs and tap at the door after you have had your dinner, Tom, I will give you a book, and introduce you to papa."

"Thank you, miss," he answered.

Miss Pringle was in the habit of attending the village church at Annerly, which was about a mile and a half distant. The way through the fields to it was a charming one, so pretty that

Tom could scarcely restrain himself and walk steadily, he wanted so much to gather wild-flowers, and chase the bees and butterflies.

His attention wandered in many directions as he sat in the free seats by the side of his mistress, until these words caught his ear: "Thou shalt not steal." They made the blood rush into his cheeks. After this his old grandmother and her lost cat occupied his thoughts. He wondered how the poor old lady would spend her Sunday without her favorite? He could not shake off the remembrance of his wicked act, and grew so uncomfortable at last, that he moved about and shuffled his feet, until he received a warning look and pinch from Miss Pringle.

He forgot his discomfort as he walked home; but then the warm sun and fresh air were so pleasant after sitting still so long, and he was to call on Mr. Newton directly after dinner, and could amuse himself in his own way until evening. One thing he decided upon, which was, to climb the castle-hill and look over to Norton Island. He could not have put his feelings into words had he tried to express them; he had a strange yearning for his own people that he had never felt before. He wanted so much to see them, for though he had only slept one night away, it seemed as if many days had passed.

Miss Pringle had roasted a shoulder of mutton on the previous afternoon to be cold for Sunday. Tom was very hungry, and glad to think the dinner would be so substantial. He helped his mistress to set the table, and took his place, wondering why she placed a morsel of dry bacon opposite to him. He soon learnt why it was there.

After Miss Pringle had cut a large plate of mutton for herself, she said, in a grave, stern voice, "You took my apples, Thomas, when I expressly ordered you not to touch one, therefore you will have no mutton today. Eat that bacon. Another time you will only have bread and water."

The boy was about to answer rudely, when conscience whispered, "You deserve the punishment; remember, you stole a peach and denied the theft;" so he kept silence.

"Your time is your own until half-past eight o'clock, Tom," said the spinster when dinner was over. "I wish you to go out at once."

"May I see Miss Annie first?" he asked.

"I suppose she will expect you; but do not be long, or you will keep me waiting."

"I can shut the door when I go out," suggested Tom.

"Indeed, you will do no such thing. I never allow my boy to be idling about the house when I am in my room. Go upstairs at once, and don't stay more than five minutes."

Tom tapped at Mr. Newton's door. It was opened by Annie. "Come in," she said. "Papa would like to see you."

They entered into conversation together, and Tom was enjoying his visit very much, when Miss Pringle knocked loudly, and asked, "How much longer do you mean to keep me waiting, Tom?"

"I musn't stay," said the boy, rising as he spoke.

"How will you spend the afternoon?" questioned Annie.

"I hardly know, miss, except that I mean to go to the castle-hill, and look at Norton Island."

"Here's a little book for you. Will you promise to read it?"

"Yes, miss, that I will."

"It's called 'Come to Jesus.' Take your Bible, and look out the texts which are referred to, and some day you shall tell me if you have accepted the invitation which Christ gives to all to come."

Tom had no Bible of his own, but did not like to confess this to his new friend; so he took the book she held out to him hastily, and said, "Good afternoon."

"You've been chattering up there too long. I hate gossiping," were the words he heard from his mistress as he entered the kitchen. "It's quite four minutes since I knocked for you to come down."

"I'm quite ready to go now," said Tom, fetching his cap.

Miss Pringle followed him to the front door, and locked it; she then retired to her bedroom, for she knew that the next two hours would be undisturbed. No visitor ever came on Sunday afternoon, and her lodgers never stirred between three and five o'clock.

But she did not read, nor did she pray, nor sleep—she spent the time in counting her sovereigns. She touched them softly, lest Mr. Newton or his daughter should hear them chink; but she touched them with a thrill of joy, for the possession of them had mastered every other feeling. She only lived to store up her money, and seemed to forget that God might one day say to her, "Thou fool, this night thy soul shall be required of thee; then whose shall those things be, which thou hast provided?"

Tom walked quietly along, sometimes peeping through the iron railing to get a better view of the bay. When he came to the gate which led to the pathway down the cliff, he sat down on the seat for a few minutes, and took out his book. As he opened it, these words arrested his attention, "If you come not to Jesus when young, it is not likely you will come at all. Habit will fasten strong chains around you, which will be harder to burst asunder every day. While you wait, Satan works. He is busy tying knots. You are his prisoner, and he is making more and more secure the cords which bind you. Whenever you sin he ties another knot."

Tom could read well, and was by no means a dull boy. "I suppose Satan tied a knot when I stole the peach, and another when I ate the apples, and I can't tell how many when I killed grandmother's cat," he said to himself.

Then he read the heading of the chapter—it was this, "Ye who are young, come." "It seems easy enough to come in a book," murmured Tom; "but it ain't easy. I'll read the chapter over again when I get on the hill. I really wish I'd a Bible of my own. I think I'll save up and buy one." He walked on until he reached Mother Crampton's house, and here he was stopped, for she was taking in some milk as he passed, and asked him where he was going to.

"The castle-hill," he replied.

"Would you like to take tea with me first, and go to the castle-hill later?" she asked.

Tom's face expressed the pleasure he felt, though he only answered, "Thank you."

The old woman and young boy became fast friends at that first tea-drinking. Tom told her what a character he had earned on the island;

how unkind he was to his brothers; how often he vexed and annoyed his parents; and he showed her his little book, and pointed to the chapter he had just read; but he did not tell her of the wrong-doing which was weighing more heavily on his conscience than all his other misdeeds.

Mother Crampton spoke very unreservedly to him, and Tom heard her with deep interest. She made it plain to him that unless he cried for mercy, the chains of sin would bind round him so tightly that he would find them hard indeed to unfasten. But he learned, too, that One was at hand to help him—One was waiting to give His spirit in answer to prayer—One was listening to catch the first faint echo of the cry, "Father, I have sinned against Heaven, and before Thee."

"Good-bye, my dear boy," said Mother Crampton at parting. "Come to me next Sunday, and instead of lounging on the castle-hill, you shall accompany me to God's house. Don't let Satan tie any more knots this week; try and unfasten the old knots, which he has been tying for so many years, by prayer. Ask in faith, and the answer will come."

"I wish—how I do wish!—I had courage to tell her all," thought Tom, as he threw himself on the turf when he reached the castle-hill. "I know I should have been a deal happier, and now I'm really right-down miserable."

CHAPTER IX.

TOM HEARS FROM HOME.

T OM, you must be off and fetch some water," said Miss Pringle the next morning. "It's very annoying, to be sure, that I should come to this. Take two pails with you."

The lad was ready to go at once, for he was anxious that the water should boil by the time Mr. Newton required it. The street was thronged as usual with water-carriers; the beautiful spring which supplied one side of Dixtown had never failed in any time of drought, and bid fair to yield so long as there was a demand. It bubbled up out of the ground, and was conducted, by means of a pipe, through a tap which was placed by the side of a fine sycamore, one of a group of six trees.

Tom had about three minute's walk to reach the spring. Just as he turned out of the house-door he saw his mother coming up the street.

After she had heard that Miss Pringle's well had failed, and where he was going to, she said, "Tell me how you're getting on."

The lad gave a detailed account of his life since he had entered on his situation, but all the time was longing to know if his mother would mention grandmother's cat. They walked towards the spring as they chatted and found when they reached it at least twelve women and children awaiting their turn to draw water.

"You must be patient, Tom," said Mrs. Gillies. "I can't stay any longer, or I shall lose the chance I have of selling my prawns by being first to cry them. I shan't be over here until Saturday, for the boys are going to have a long turn, and I've a deal of setting to rights to do at home. I don't think I've any news to tell you. O, yes! I have. I declare I quite forgot it in seeing you and hearing about Miss Pringle. Grandmother's lost her cat."

"Lost her cat, mother! What do you mean?" asked Tom, trying to keep his color down, and stopping to pick up one of the pails, which he kicked over because he felt he must do something.

"Why, I mean that Tabby's dead; and how the poor creature came to run into the sea nobody can tell. Sally thinks she fell over the cliff, and that the crabs attacked her, for she had a great hole in one side, and Sally saw a big crab scuttling away."

"How came Sally to see the cat?"

"She went to look after grandmother who was out in that terrible storm the day before you left, as you know; and she found her very low because Tabby hadn't come home, so Sally went after the cat, and saw her lying dead on the shore and Dick carried her home and helped bury her in the garden; and grandmother says she'll never have another favorite. But I musn't stay any longer. Good-bye, Tom."

The boy gave a great sigh of relief as his mother left him, because his secret was safe. Then he thought of the knots. It wasn't the way to get rid of sin to try and hide it; and with all his efforts he couldn't hide it from God. He was so occupied with his thoughts he did not notice that he was alone at the spring. He filled his pails quickly, and made such haste home that the water was boiling before Annie came down-stairs to fill her teapot.

In the afternoon Miss Pringle ordered him to take a basket and gather some blackberries from the hedges in Windmill Lane where she heard they were hanging in thick, ripe bunches. "You may pick a good few, Tom," she said, "for the apples are falling, but will do very well for jam, mixed with blackberries."

Tom liked the idea of a run in the lanes, but was barely out of sight of the house before he was stopped by hearing the whistle he knew so well, and turning round, found that Dick Potter was close behind him.

"What have you come to Dixtown for?" asked Tom.

"Because I've got no one to go out with on Norton Island, now you've gone, and I've nothing to do at the quarries, for I've quarreled with the foreman," answered Dick; "and father was so angry he sent me off to find work at the harbor. I've been waiting about here since one o'clock for you to come out. Where are you going to?"

Tom told his errand.

"I'll go with you, and help you," said his friend.

As the boys walked to Windmill Lane Dick enlarged on the untimely end of grandmother's cat. Tom winced several times when he alluded to the poor old woman's sorrow; but he made no confidant of his companion, and right glad was he to reach the blackberries in order to turn the conversation into another channel.

"Here we are," he said, interrupting Dick in the middle of a sentence. "How splendid they are! Now let's go to work."

The basket was soon filled and then the boys feasted themselves.

"What are you going to do?" asked Tom as they came almost within sight of Miss Pringle's house.

"I shall lounge about until dark and share your bed to-night," answered Dick.

"But you can't. Miss Pringle will never let you."

"I don't mean to ask her. I'm coming at your invitation."

"But I can't give you one. Why don't you ask some of your friends at the harbor?"

"After to-night I will. Do, Tom, there's a good fellow, let me sleep with you just for once. I'll go away before daylight. I'm promised work for to-morrow, so it's only to-night."

"But I can't get you in, Dick. Miss Pringle locks as well as bolts the doors and carries the keys in her pocket."

"You're a stupid fellow, Tom. Can't a fellow come in other ways besides through a door? There's a window at the back I suppose."

"Yes, in the kitchen."

"Where do you sleep?"

"Under the staircase. There's only just room for me. I'm sure you couldn't get in as well," said Tom, in a dolorous voice.

"I shall try, at any rate. Now, Tom, don't be disagreeable. I know you'll put yourself out for an old chum. I'd do as much for you. I shall be

taken on to-morrow; and the fisherman says
he'll pay me every day just at first. So I only
want your help for this one night."

When Dick coaxed, Tom was sure to yield.
As we have said, his was not a strong character,
nor had he strong principles; so he finally
yielded to his friend's evil influence.

"As it's only one night, Dick," he said, "I
don't so much mind; but you must come in
very carefully, for there are lodgers in the
house, and Miss Pringle sleeps over the
kitchen. If she finds me out, she'll give me over
to a policeman."

"Don't be frightened, Tom, but trust me to
take care of myself and you too. I'll tap at the
kitchen window when the clock beings to strike
ten."

Dick had invented a tissue of falsehoods. He
had not quarreled with Mr. Pender's foreman,
nor had he a situation in prospect. The truth
was he had no work at the quarries for two
days, and thought he might as well go over to
Dixtown to see how Tom fared and he intended
returning to Norton Island on the following
morning. Mr. Potter never troubled himself
about his son, and Dick had no mother. His
step-mother was a kind-hearted woman, but
had a large family to care for and she was
rather relieved than otherwise when her stepson
absented himself from home, for she disliked

his idle habits, and feared that his evil influence would be hurtful to her children.

Miss Pringle was satisfied with her basket of blackberries, but Tom was not satisfied with himself. As he peeled the apples he thought of Mother Crampton's advice, "Don't let Satan tie any more knots this week." "I know I'm going to tie a big one to-night," he said aloud, forgetting how near Miss Pringle was to him.

"I didn't hear you, Tom," called his mistress. "I'd just gone out of the garden door for a moment. What did you say?"

Tom started, and felt very foolish. Fortunately Annie Newton came in from a walk at this moment, and hearing voices in the kitchen, looked in to ask him how he liked his book.

"Pretty well, thank you," he stammered out, but seemed so uncomfortable that she did not venture to ask a second question.

Every half hour that passed made Tom more miserable. He wished that he could break his rash promise, but he dare not, for he knew that Dick would be noisy if so treated. When the clock chimed a quarter to ten he left his bed, and made his way into the kitchen. He was not a coward by nature, but the sense of wrong-doing sometimes makes the stoutest heart fail. A mouse nibbled in the wainscot as he passed, and frightened him so much that he broke out

into a cold perspiration. The moonlight
streamed in over the top of the shutters, and
reflected his own shadow on the wall, and he
trembled. Still he went forward, and unfastened
the shutter gently, just in time to see Dick glide
up the garden, under the shelter of the wall. He
had entered through the fields, which extended
for some distance, and were only separated
from the garden by a low hedge.

The window was soon unbolted, and in a few
moments Dick was standing in the kitchen.
"I'm so glad to be here," he said, "so very glad!
You're a good fellow, Tom. Let me go to bed
at once, and mind you wake me early to-
morrow. I'm sure to sleep on, for I'm so tired."

"I don't know how you're to get into my bed;
it's scarcely big enough for one," whispered
Tom.

"Let me stay here. The floor will do for me.
Show me where you sleep."

"Follow me," replied Tom. "But come very
gently."

The two boys groped their way to the
staircase. Dick had a box of lucifers with him,
and a candle, which he lighted, for Miss
Pringle took good care that Tom should not be
supplied with either article.

"I see there's only room for one," said Dick,
after he had looked into the hole which Miss
Pringle called a bedroom. "I'd just as soon be

in the kitchen. You go to bed now, and I'll come to you if I wake first; but I dare say I shall sleep latest."

Tom returned to his bed somewhat comforted. Dick behaved so well that he was almost glad he had let him in, and perhaps no harm would come of it. He listened for a few minutes, to assure himself that all was still ere he fell asleep.

Dick could hardly have explained the reason why he was so anxious to make his way into Miss Pringle's house, beyond it being a cheap mode of getting a roof over his head for the night; and he liked the fun and excitement of it. He was about to settle himself for he night, when he heard a great noise overhead, which startled Miss Pringle as much as Dick, so fearful was she of exciting suspicion; in her passage to the cupboard she had tumbled over a chair.

"What can the old maid be after?" he thought. "I'll go and see."

He soon slipped off his boots, and crept up the stairs. He looked through the keyhole, and was astonished at the sight it revealed. Miss Pringle was sitting on a chair facing door, so that he could see every movement. Having assured herself that no alarm was raised, she turned a number of sovereigns out of a stocking into her lap, and having counted them carefully, returned them one by one into the stocking and deposited the stocking in a wooden box. She managed to do this so quietly that he scarcely heard the chink of money. There was no sound in the house, save the regular breathing of one asleep in the lodger's room, so Dick kept his post until he had mastered the spinster's secret, and learned that the bandbox in her cupboard did not contain her best bonnet.

He returned to the kitchen as quietly as he had left it, and lay down on the hard floor. It was a long time before he could forget himself in sleep. At last it came, but there was little refreshment in it, for he dreamed of gold, gold, nothing but gold. He was reaching out his hand to grasp the coveted treasure when Tom shook him. "Get up, Dick," he said; "you must be off or she'll see you. You've been moaning so, I was afraid you'd be heard. You've been dreaming hard."

"I think I have," answered Dick, rubbing his eyes, and gradually awaking to a sense of passing events.

"Be quick and go. I don't want to get into a scrape," urged Tom.

Dick was soon ready, and Tom was extremely relieved when he lost sight of him.

CHAPTER X.

THE EXCURSION TO LOCKSTONE.

DICK returned to Norton Island that afternoon and went to work at the quarries on the following morning. He thought of nothing all day but the bright sovereigns he had seen Miss Pringle handle so carefully; if he had so many how he would enjoy himself; money commanded everything, and it was hard that so much should lie idle at the top of an old woman's cupboard. At last he envied Tom his situation, for if he had lived with Miss Pringle he might have had some chance of getting at her hoard. Yet Dick knew there was only one way of possessing it, and that was to steal. He did not want to risk imprisonment, but if sure of escaping detection, he would have been glad enough to get the money into his hands.

When Saturday came he resolved to go Dixtown. Tom would shelter him again. He could be persuaded to do anything. "And if," said Dick to himself, "if I see my way clear to turn him out, and turn myself in, I'll do it." As his plans were uncertain he told his step-mother that there was no chance of work at the quarries for a week, so he meant to try after a job at Dixtown harbor, and might be absent several days.

It was late in the afternoon before Dick was able to get a lift over to Dixtown. Just as he reached the high street he spied Tom in the distance, who had been to the grocer's for his mistress. "How lucky I am to come across you so soon," said Dick, tapping his friend on the shoulder. "I'm here on purpose to see you."

Tom did not appear very glad to meet Dick. "I thought you'd got a situation," he said.

"It ended in smoke. I've been home, but felt so dull without you, I've come back. We'll have an afternoon together to-morrow, and go to Lockstone to fish. The tide will just suit us to walk there and back on the sands. I'll sleep in the kitchen to-night as I did before."

Tom's face fell. "I can't let you in again, Dick," he said, but in a hesitating tone of voice. "I really can't, it's so risky; and I daren't go out with you tomorrow, for if we were to be late home, Miss Pringle would send me away."

"Stuff, Tom, as if a boy like you, who knows every turn of the tide, is likely to be late. They say Lockstone is splendid, and it's quite a short walk by the sands; and it's a new place for both of us. You will enjoy a run after being shut up all the week."

Dick could act the part of tempter to perfection, and Tom was not proof against his wiles. "If I was sure we should get home in time, I shouldn't mind going," he answered.

"Of course you will; I'll take good care of that."

"But I can't let you sleep in the kitchen, Dick, even if I do go to Lockstone."

"What nonsense, Tom, I think you're turning quite silly. Expect me at ten o'clock," and Dick walked quickly away in the opposite direction. The above conversation gave him food for thought. It was evident that Tom was afraid of forfeiting his place if he were after time on Sunday evening. Why could he not devise some means to keep him out so late that Miss Pringle would dismiss him, and then he might apply for the situation?

Tom admitted him as before, but this time they were in fear of detection, for Dick stumbled and fell, and the noise he made must have been heard by Miss Pringle, had she not at that moment been standing on a high stool inside the cupboard. Tom shook in every limb, and even his companion was frightened. They listened for some minutes, but all was perfectly still, so Tom went to his bed, and Dick pretended to lie down. The latter made several attempts to go up stairs, but every time he came near to Tom he heard him moving, so he dare not; and when he felt that he might venture because Tom was snoring, all was dark and still in Miss Pringle's room.

Tom breathed a sigh of relief when Dick was out of the house next morning; but he no longer had misgivings about the excursion to Lockstone, for his friend had dilated on their prospective enjoyment until he fully entered into the plan. He was well pleased, too, that Dick did not ask him if he might sleep there a second night; he had said at parting, "I shan't come again Tom, for I see it worries you. I think I know a fellow who will give me a bed, just for once."

Tom accompanied his mistress to church, but his thoughts were at Lockstone, and occupied in making arrangements which had reference to his afternoon outing. He was a little puzzled to make up his mind whether he had better tell Mother Crampton he was engaged to Dick and could not stay to tea with her, or make an excuse when he saw her. He decided on the latter course.

So soon as dinner was over he went to his room and put on his every-day suit quietly, and taking his cap he walked down the passage to

the front door without going into the kitchen
again.

Miss Pringle heard him, and called out,
"Mind you're home punctually, Tom." To
which he replied, "I'll be here."

"You're very exact to time," said Dick, who
was waiting just out of sight. "I've brought a
net with me, for we may as well catch some
fish, and I begged a loaf in case we should be
hungry, from a fisherman I know."

The day was warm and fine, and when the
boys were fairly on the way their spirits rose,
and they laughed and talked gaily. Though the
tide was running out they had to climb over
high boulders, and scale deep pools in order to
get along. Lockstone Point was about two
miles from Dixtown; it ran out from some
distance into the sea, and was formed of rocks
of all shapes and sizes, tilted up on edge. Some
of them made little islands, round which the
waves splashed and foamed, and all of them
were thickly covered with mussels; while the
deep pools were rich in corallines, anemones,
seaweed, and crustacean of every description.
Tom forgot it was Sunday; forgot his
conversation with Mother Crampton; forgot
that he was tying, and not untying, knots;
forgot all but a sense of intense enjoyment, at
once more returning to his old life.

It was five o'clock before they reached the Point, for they loitered by the way, trying to catch shrimps and turning over the great jelly fish that were strewn about the sands. At Lockstone they found full grown crabs, and netted so many prawns in the pools that they each had enough tied up in their pocket-handkerchiefs to furnish a large dish.

"We musn't stay here too long," said Tom. "I think we'd better be off now. We shall have nice time to get up the cliffs by the pathway yonder, and home by the lanes, without hurrying ourselves."

"We've lots of time to walk by the shore," replied Dick.

"I tell you I'd rather not venture," answered Tom.

"And I tell you it's nonsense. I hate the lanes; there's nothing to do; and there's no end of amusement by the sea. Come along, I'll lead the way."

Tom thought it looked very tempting.

"Be quick," shouted Dick. "There's plenty of time if you come directly. The tide isn't nearly up."

Still Tom hesitated, but finally allowed himself, as usual, to be led as his companion willed.

"All right," he said, "but mind I'm going ahead. I'm not going to stop and dawdle about."

Dick allowed him to have his way until he has passed one or two difficulties in the shape of jutting points of rock, which was covered by the waves at high water; and then he began to call Tom's attention to one object after another. At length they reached a cave with a deep pool in it, and a narrow ledge of rock on either side.

"Let's go along here," said Dick; "we shall find plenty of crags in the crevices of the rock."

Tom had not noticed the cave on the way to Lockstone, and it offered great attractions to him, so he walked along the narrow ledge, followed by his friend. When they had penetrated so far in as was prudent, and were turning round to go back again, Dick, apparently by accident, but really intentionally, tripped him up, and sent him sprawling into the water. He had some difficulty in scrambling out again, and was thoroughly wet through. Dick pretended to be very sorry, and helped him to take off his coat and waistcoat. The tide was coming in faster than either of them knew. Dick only discovered it just in time to warn Tom, and drag him, coat and waistcoat in hand, on to a place of safety, when a great wave dashed in, and covered the ledge on which they had been standing five minutes before.

"We're well out of that," exclaimed Dick. "I don't know where it would have swept us to."

The boys were now on a rock out of reach of the water; it was a point rarely covered, except in time of storm, and it stood at the base of a perpendicular cliff.

"Here's a pretty go," called out Tom, who had been looking anxiously, first on one side, and then on the other. "I believe we're tide-bound."

"That we are," answered his companion. "We certainly can't pass the next point. I don't care about myself, but I'm sorry for you, because of Miss Pringle." And Dick really looked quite vexed, though he was secretly rejoicing over the great success of his plan.

Tom's face expressed his disappointment. "How stupid I was not to go straight up from Lockstone," he said. "It's your fault, Dick, for persuading me to come back by the shore."

"It's yours, Tom, for you fell into the pool, and hindered our getting on."

Nothing was to be gained by quarrelling for it was impossible to pass the points on either side, and there was no way up the cliff between Lockstone and a fishing village close to Dixtown, so Tom was obliged to wait.

"Don't put on your coat, old fellow," said Dick. "Dry it now. I declare, here's a tiny cave just below; let's creep into it, and sleep here."

"No, that I won't," answered Tom, resolutely. "I'm sure it isn't eight o'clock; by ten the tide may have turned enough for us to get on again."

"Miss Pringle will never let you in. Fancy her sitting up for you."

"I'll try at any rate, whatever you may say," replied Tom, angrily.

"Don't put yourself into a temper," retorted Dick. "You shall have your own way; but I say she won't let you in."

It was after midnight when they reached Dixtown. They were far out in their calculations of the tide, for they really knew nothing of the state of the shore on that side of the bay. Dick accompanied Tom to Miss Pringle's house, and waited to see if he could gain admission. He knocked once, twice, and thrice, before Mr. Newton opened his window, and said, "I'm sorry I can't let you in, but Miss Pringle has forbidden it.'

"Come along, we shall find an empty boat by the harbor, Tom. It's no use attempting to get in anywhere. It won't be the first time in your life that you've slept in the open air." And Dick led the way, followed by his crest-fallen companion.

CHAPTER XI.

HOW TOM FARED.

TOM was very miserable when he awoke. Dick was not by his side, and he had evidently slept until a late hour. He tried to rouse himself and stand up, but he felt very weak and ill. He was sitting, with his head between his hands, thinking of the last night's catastrophe, when Dick appeared, carrying a bundle. The boys had not slept in a boat, but under an archway in the cliff.

"Tom, old boy," said his friend, "I've been doing my best for you. I woke up early, and as you were still asleep I thought I'd do you a good turn with Miss Pringle, so I went to her and said I was to blame for taking you out, and I asked her to forgive you this once. Then I told her how sorry you were, and how the state of the tide deceived us both."

"Well, what did she say?" asked Tom.

"She won't take you back on no account. She made me wait while she packed your clothes, and told me to tell you that you'd better go home."

"I'll never do that," replied Tom, angrily; "but I wish, Dick, you'd minded your own business, and left me to manage mine."

"I do call that unkind. It's not like you, Tom; but it never answers to help a fellow out of a scrape."

"I think I'll go and beg her pardon, at any rate. Don't you be vexed, Dick; I suppose you meant to be kind. Give me a helping hand."

When Tom stood up, he was so giddy that he was glad to lie down again. "I can't go," he said, piteously, "I fell so ill. Mother is going \to Miss Pringle this morning with my clothes; ask her to come here."

Dick was very glad to be thus dismissed, in order to escape further questioning from Tom. And now we must inform our readers of the substance of the conversation which took place between him and the spinster, when he went, as he said, to do his friend a good turn. He had waited until the harbor clock struck six, and, rejoicing that Tom still slept, he ran to Miss Pringle's house. She was sweeping her shop, and grumbling meanwhile at having to do it herself. Dick rang the outside bell. She went hastily to the door, her face wearing its most severe expression; and, to her astonishment, she saw a strange boy. Miss Pringle had

resolved to keep Tom for the six months. In
many respects he suited her, and she had even
once or twice entertained the idea of giving
him a shilling a week at the end of half a year,
for he appeared, on the whole, to fit in better
than any boy she had had before; but Tom must
show signs of repentance, and be severely
punished for his disobedience. She considered
turning him adrift into the streets for the night
would be wholesome discipline; and hence she
told Annie not to admit him if he knocked and
rang twenty times, for he should never enter
her house again.

"Who are you?" Miss Pringle asked when she
saw the strange boy at her door.

"I'm Tom Gillie's friend," said Dick. "I've
called for his clothes; he ain't coming back
again; he don't' take to the baking business."

"Impertinent boy!" exclaimed the spinster,
angrily. "How dare he treat me so rudely! I'll
complain to his mother."

"They can't do nothing with him at home,"
said Dick, in a plausible tone. "He didn't ought
to behave so to you. I'm sure other boys would
be glad to live here."

"Certainly," replied Miss Pringle. "I really
cannot understand Tom; he mentioned nothing
to me about leaving yesterday."

"He was so angry because you didn't let him
in last night, and made him sleep under the

archway; he says it was barbarous of you, and you oughtn't to have treated him so badly."

"Oh, that's the way he talks about his wicked behavior; he wishes to turn the tables on me, I suppose. You may take his clothes away; but it's very annoying to be left without a boy."

"I suppose I shouldn't do?" said Dick, looking very humble. "I should like to live with you."

"What's your name?"

"Dick Potter. I came from Norton Island."

"If I take you I must learn something about your parents. I have known Mrs. Gillies for many years, but I do not know your mother."

"I haven't got a mother of my own," said Dick, rubbing his eyes with the back of his hand. "Mother died years ago, and father's married again, and there's a lot of children at home."

"When could you come to me?"

"To-day; for I'm sure Mr. Pender would let me off at once. I only get odd jobs to do at the quarries, and I do want reg'lar work."

"If you live with me you will have to work hard; I cannot have lazy people here. Tom did his work well if he liked. Are you certain he sent you for his clothes?"

"Quite certain, Miss Pringle. If you'd heard what shameful language he used about you,

I'm sure you'd have sent them away, even if I hadn't come after them."

"I thought you were his friend," said the spinster, sharply.

"So I am, for we've been brought up together, I might almost say; but, for all that, I like justice to be done to people who's as kind to 'em as you've been to Tom."

"Time was fast slipping away, and Miss Pringle had to bake her bread; she had hoped Tom would return in time to light the fire. "Wait a moment while I fetch the clothes," she said, "for I must make my bread at once, or I shall be behind all day."

She went to the drawers, and then discovered that Tom had worn his every-day suit. "Deceitful boy!" she muttered; "he must have been bent on mischief or he would not have changed his clothes secretly. I'm sure he's no loss."

"There is the bundle," she said, giving it to Dick; "if you like to take it to Tom, and return to me, I will see how you can work."

"I shan't be long," replied Dick.

Soon after the bundle of clothes was dispatched Mrs. Gillies called to see her son, and heard an exaggerated account of his behavior from Miss Pringle. She scarcely heeded her last works, "I've got another boy in his place," but started away to find Tom, for the spinster could give her no information as to his whereabouts. She met Dick, who directed her; but he did not tell her whither he was going, and she was so full of seeking for Tom, she did not remark on the strangeness of meeting him in the town at that early hour.

"A pretty state of things!" she said, angrily, when she found her son. "You'll ruin yourself, Tom, and your father will be terribly vexed. I don't know what to do with you. I suppose you must go back home with me. Will is coming over in his boat at two o'clock, so get up and don't lie idly there. I'll ask Mother Crampton to let you sit in her chimney corner until I'm ready, and the boat's here."

Tom tried to rise, but could not steady himself without his mother's help, he was so stiff and giddy.

"Here's a bad boy come to sit in your kitchen, Mother Crampton," said Mrs. Gillies, dragging her son in. "He's been up to some of his old games, and Miss Pringle's sent him off."

Tom looked so miserable that the Dame made no remark. She had imagined something was amiss when he did not keep his appointment on the previous afternoon.

"He's welcome to stay here," she replied.

"Then I'm off," said Mrs. Gillies. "I shall be back long before two o'clock. Sit by the fire, Tom, and don't stand shivering there."

Mother Crampton had no time to ask any questions for the first hour, but when her bed was made, and her room tidied, she put the breakfast things on a round table near the fire, with a loaf and butter.

Tom sat with his head in his hands, and took no notice; he felt very much ashamed, and fancied he was very ill.

"Come, my boy, cheer up," said Mother Crampton; "drink a cup of tea, eat the thin slice of bread and butter I'm cutting for you, and then tell me all about yesterday."

By degrees she drew from Tom, the history of his Sunday excursion with Dick, and why he had not come to see her.

"I'm very sorry to hear all this," she remarked, when he ceased speaking. "Oh, Tom, you've been tying and not untying knots all the week. I did so hope you were going to turn over a new leaf. I really am very much grieved and disappointed."

Tom's tears began to fall fast. If Mother Crampton had scolded, he could have borne it better than her kind, earnest words.

"But it really was all Dick's fault," he sobbed. "I shouldn't have thought about going to Lockstone if he hadn't asked me."

"But not his fault that you yielded to the temptation. If you succumb to every unholy influence that you meet with in this world, you will heap up sorrow here and hereafter."

"I never have been so wretched in all my life, except"—and Tom stopped, for he thought of grandmother's cat, and this made him remember that he was going home, and would see her. "I can't, I really can't," he added aloud, "I can't go home, Mother Crampton, for she—I mean, they'll all be so angry with me."

"You must bear it as part of the punishment you have brought on yourself. You are not well enough to take another situation directly; but I will promise you, that if at the end of a week I hear a good character of you, and your cold is gone, you shall come and stay here until I find you something to do."

Tom's eyes brightened. "That'll make them kinder to me," he said. "Father told me never to show my face there again if I didn't stay with Miss Pringle; but perhaps he won't be so angry if I tell him what you say."

"Deeds, not words, my boy," said Mother Crampton, drinking her last cup of tea. "I'll stop over the way, for I fancy neighbor Driver may want a boy to help in his bakehouse."

Tom's face fell. "I'd rather be anything than a baker's boy," he exclaimed. Then checking himself, he added, "I'll do my best to be good.

If only Dick Potter will keep clear of me I shan't mind. Miss Pringle will tell you that I tried hard to please her, though once or twice I was very wicked," for Tom remembered the peach and apples.

"You must try and be good, Tom, because you serve a great King. "It's no use for you to think that you'll be different if away from Dick's influence; you must pray that strength may come to enable you to endure temptation, as a good soldier of Christ."

Mother Crampton had put away her last tea-cup, when a tap came at the door; the latch was lifted up, and a fresh-colored woman with a good-natured face looked in. "Good morning, Mother," she said, in a friendly, cheery voice. "I've just stepped over to tell you that my Jack has given us up, for he's had an offer to better himself in a gentleman's family; so if you hear of a steady boy who'll ride our horses, and take out the vegetables, I shall be glad. I'd rather not have a Dixtown boy, for I don't want him to be running off home at all hours. He must sleep under the counter, and do any odd jobs that are wanted. He's treated like one of the family if he behaves himself. I can't stay, for there's nobody to mind the shop." And, without adding another word, Mrs. Jones closed the door.

Tom had risen in his excitement, and he looked very wistful. "Oh, Mother Crampton, do you think she'd have me? I will try so hard to please her, she's so different from Miss Pringle," he said.

"It really does seem a lucky thing, and yet there's no such thing as luck, Tom," replied the old woman, thoughtfully. "I believe, my dear, it's God helping you. I'll go and say a word for you at once."

The boy sat in great anxiety, and thought Mother Crampton would never come back. She and her opposite neighbor were on very friendly terms. Mrs. Jones was a young married woman with two children. Her husband kept a greengrocer's shop, and had six bathing machines besides. She superintended the shop in the morning when the bathing season commenced, while Mr. Jones and his boy were attending to the bathers. They had a good vegetable and fruit garden one mile out of Dixtown, but they lived over the shop. They were kind-hearted, honest, and hard-working people, who highly appreciated good Mother Crampton.

The dame did not find it very difficult to induce Mrs. Jones to give Tom a trial, though she told her much of his past history. "I'd take him to please you," said the greengrocer's wife; "send him over here at one o'clock, husband will be at home then."

Tom almost forgot his illness and misery when Mother Crampton returned with such good news. He brushed his hair, and washed his hands, and waited anxiously for one o'clock to strike.

Mr. Jones was pleased with him, he appeared so desirous of finding a situation, and answered the questions he was asked in a straightforward manner; so he was engaged to come for a month on trial, at the rate of three shillings a week, and his food and lodging.

It seemed like a fortune to Tom.

"Mind, boy," said Mr. Jones as he was leaving, "I won't have yesterday's behavior repeated. Mother Crampton has told my missus all about it. If you play truant, I'll turn you out neck and crop—no Sunday gadding here. We treat our boy well, and expect him to attend church, and walk out with us and the children on fine afternoons. You may go over and see Mother Crampton sometimes; and I'll give you a holiday home from Saturday until Monday once in six months."

Tom could only keep reiterating, "Thank you, sir," and pulling the front lock of his hair, until it was a wonder he did not pull it out.

"When shall I be wanted?" he asked.

"Let's see—Jack goes on Monday. Come a week to-morrow," answered Mr. Jones.

"O, Mother Crampton! How can I thank you enough?" said Tom, rushing into the room. "I'm engaged, and I'm going to get three shillings a week. Oh, how jolly! How jolly!"

"You seem wonderful better," said Mrs. Gillies, whom Tom had not perceived in his excitement.

"Yes, I am, mother, for I'm so happy. Only think—I'm to have three shillings a week. Father won't be angry to see me," and he clapped his hands and danced about with pleasure.

Mother Crampton found an opportunity of whispering in his ear before he left, "My boy, if you wish to show your gratitude to me, you will begin to pray."

"I promise you I will," replied Tom; and so they parted.

"Hallo! How is it you're back, like a bad penny?" Will, who was waiting at the harbor, asked his brother.

"I'm only come for a holiday," said Tom looking very red.

"Has Miss Pringle been so handsome as to let you off so soon?"

"Tom isn't going back to Miss Pringle," answered Mrs. Gillies. "He's going to a place where he'll get good victuals and three shillings a week."

Mother Crampton had entreated her not to scold Tom. "Make the best of it," she said. "The boy has had a bad companion in Dick Potter; let us see what we can do by treating him as if he were not worse than others. I like him with all his faults, and I mean to be his friend."

Tom's appearance at home caused some excitement; but after his father had heard his wife's version of the story, and his three elder brothers had put their questions, he was allowed to remain in peace, and thoroughly enjoyed the tea and fish, of which the whole family partook. He was telling them about his life with Miss Pringle, when three taps came at the door which made his blood run cold, for they told him that grandmother was there. She looked annoyed to see him. "Just as I expected," she said, contemptuously. "You'll never stay anywhere. You're a bad, worthless boy."

"Gently, gently, granny," said Mrs. Gillies. "Tom has come home for a holiday. He's bettered himself, and is going to live with Mr. Jones, the greengrocer, now."

"Oh, that's it, is it? Well, it doesn't matter to me where he goes, so that he isn't idling about the island with Dick Potter. I called to see if one of the boys would come over to-morrow morning. I've had a willow given to me for poor Tabby's grave," and here the old woman's voice trembled a little—"and I want it planted, and the fuchsia that's there now put in the garden."

"I'll come in the evening," said Will, "but I shan't have time in the morning. We go away fishing first thing."

"I dare say the evening will do just as well," replied granny, "for the tree has a good root; it won't die if it's left out of the ground another day."

"May I come to you in the morning?" Tom ventured to say. "I can dig as well as the boys."

"You!" exclaimed Old Mrs. Gillies, in a voice that stung Tom. "As if I should ask *you* to do anything for me. Will, do not forget your promise. Good-bye all."

"Granny will never like you, Tom, that's quite certain," remarked Harry, rising from the table as he spoke. "Come, Will, we must see to our nets, and get ready for tomorrow."

Tom was miserable again. He followed his mother into the kitchen, and said, "I'll go to bed, for I feel as if I were beginning to shiver again."

"I would if I were you," she answered, kindly. "A long night will do you a deal of good."

Tom prayed his first earnest prayer before he undressed. The words he said were somewhat rambling, but they came from his heart. Then he crept into his corner of the room, and was soon so fast asleep, that he did not hear his little brothers come to bed.

The next morning he felt much better, and could not resist a great desire that possessed him to see Tabby's grave; yet he did not wish to meet his grandmother. He walked along the shore so as not to be seen approaching by her, and clambered up the cliff close to the door of the cottage; but his precautions availed nothing, for granny caught sight of him, and called out, "What are you prowling about here for, Tom? You never do any one credit. It shows how bad you are for Miss Pringle to send you away and take Dick in your place."

"What do you mean?" asked Tom in astonishment. "Who told you Dick was going to live with Miss Pringle?"

"He told me so himself last night. I met him on my way home after I'd seen you. He came over to fetch his clothes. I heard a few things about you from him."

"I'll fight him for telling lies. I know he's played me false," said Tom; and, without waiting to think, he ran off to find his former friend.

Mrs. Potter was busy washing when Tom entered her cottage, and asked, in a very unceremonious manner, "Where's Dick?"

"Gone to his new situation. How was it you didn't suit Miss Pringle, Tom?"

"I did suit her until Dick interfered," replied the lad, more quietly, for Mrs. Potter had asked the question very kindly.

"I hope you will soon find another place."

"I've got one already," replied Tom, and his face cleared. "I'm glad not go to back and live with Miss Pringle; but I hate to be so badly treated as Dick's treated me."

Mrs. Potter would have probably encouraged Tom to give his version of the story, had she not been very busy, and really intensely relieved to think that her stepson had gone to live a little distance off.

Tom had so much food for thought, he forgot all about his desire to see Tabby's grave, and sat on a rock wondering however Dick managed to ingratiate himself into Miss Pringle's good graces.

"If I find he's played me false, I'll fight him, that I will," he said aloud.

"And tie another knot," Tom seemed to hear.

"No, I won't do that," he said, as if answering someone who spoke. "I'll pray instead. After all, I've got the best of the bargain, and I know

I don't deserve it. How I wish I was good, like Miss Annie and Mother Crampton.

When Tom returned home, he found his sister alone, for the little ones were at school, and his mother gone to Dixtown. They had a long talk together, and Sally was deeply interested in all that he told her about his new friends; he read to her the chapter from "Come to Jesus," entitled, "Ye who are young, Come," and she said she should remember the words about tying fresh knots.

"I'll buy you a book like mine, Sally," said Tom, "as soon as I get my first wages, and I mean to buy myself a Bible. Have you got one?"

"Yes, of course I have; don't you remember I had it for a prize from Mr. Pender while I was at school."

Mrs. Gillies returned from Dixtown late in the afternoon, and found Tom sitting quietly at home, telling his little brothers and sisters a story.

"What do you say to Dick having gone to live with Miss Pringle?" she asked him.

"He's played me false, mother; but after all, he's done me good. Have you spoken to him?"

"Certainly I have. He looks very meek indeed; and Miss Pringle says she never had such a boy; but new brooms sweep clean. Dick has only been tried for a few hours. He sent his love to you."

"I'd rather not have it. Did you tell him, mother, I'd got another situation?"

"Yes; I couldn't help it."

"What did he say?"

"Not much; but I thought he looked rather vexed when he heard you were to have three shillings a week."

"I'm off to grandmother, Tom," said Will, looking in at the door. "You may as well come and help me."

Tom was glad to accompany his brother, though granny scowled when she saw him. "I want his help," explained Will.

"Oh, very well," she replied, "then I've nothing more to say. I know it seems nonsense to you for me to make all this fuss about a cat's grave," she continued, when Will began removing the shells; "but I loved Tabby so much. I declare, I looked for her to meet me just as your mother looks out for you. A lone woman takes to dumb animals. I never returned home without wondering if she was watching for me to come."

"Why don't you get another, granny?" asked Will.

"I'd rather not. I don't want to love another as I loved poor Tabby."

Tom felt very guilty, and was thoroughly glad when all was in order again. He applied himself to place the shells with such exactness, that he won thanks from grandmother on leaving.

"I can't have the big knot I tied when I killed Tabby forever on my shoulders," he thought, when he was alone. "I'll make up my mind to buy grandmother a handsome kitten with my first wages, and it shall have a red collar. I'll tell Mother Crampton, that I will, and ask her opinion. Perhaps she'll advise me to confess to granny how wicked I have been; but I don't know how I ever shall, for she downright hates me now."

CHAPTER XII.

QUITE BLIND.

WHILE the events we have narrated in the last two chapters occurred, Annie Newton was passing through deep waters. Her father's health, as we know, had been declining for some time, and his eyesight was sorely affected. She would have entered into the question of Tom's dismissal with more earnestness, had she been differently situated; but on the very Monday when Dick acted so falsely, Mr. Newton awoke to blindness.

"Annie, child," he called from his bed, "I can't see this morning."

The young girl was quickly at his side.

"What is the matter, papa?" she asked, for she only heard the accents of pain, but did not distinguish the words.

"I'm blind—I can't see you, darling."

"Perhaps you will be better presently, papa," she replied. "I will get breakfast ready, and fetch you some warm water, and you shall bathe your eyes."

She was soon on her way down stairs, but found, to her discomfort, that the kitchen fire was only just lighted, and that Miss Pringle was very cross.

"You must wait for your water, miss," she said. "It's too bad of Tom Gillies to treat me like this. He's sent for his clothes, and won't come back again."

Annie was so pre-occupied that she scarcely noticed Miss Pringle's remark about Tom, but answered, "Papa is so ill this morning that I want to get him some breakfast at once."

"The water will boil in five minutes. You must be patient, Miss Annie."

"I suppose I must; but I am really very much troubled, Miss Pringle. I shall return to papa, and come back again for my water."

"She's only a child in behavior, and ought to know better than be so full of her own affairs, and never think of my worries," said the spinster to herself. "I wonder if that new boy will suit me. It's intensely vexing, to be sure, to be left in this manner by Tom. I really began to like him." And Miss Pringle vented her spleen on the chairs and tables, and knocked and thumped her furniture, and banged the doors, and poked the fire noisily. She was glad to see Dick; and he set to work so heartily that he

soon made up for lost time. When Annie came
down the second time, he was receiving orders
from his mistress. She could not help noticing
his face—it struck her as so opposite to Tom's;
but she asked no questions then, for her father
appeared so prostrate, she scarcely liked to
leave him for a few minutes. He seemed better
able to talk after he had taken a cup of tea, and
called her to his side.

"I'm quite blind, Annie darling," he
murmured. "Quite blind; it's come at last. God
help you!" And he sobbed, as only a man can
sob when hope dies out for the moment, and he
thinks of those whose lives depend on his
exertions for support.

Annie came to her father's side. "Papa, dear,
God will help us—we shall not be left," she
said.

"I'm so disappointed, child. I felt so much
better yesterday, and yet I knew it must come
at last. How I shall miss the blue sky and the
fields and trees. But I must not forget; there is a
land beyond, where I shall see again."

"Yes, dear father, try and think of that land,
and then you will have strength to bear
anything that comes."

"Draw nearer to me, Annie; put your face
between my hands; let me know your features
by feeling them. I did so love to look at you."

"I will try very hard to be eyes to you, papa. I will take you out, and tell you about everything I see. I can pick up the shells we require quite well now.'

"Ah! That is another trouble, dearest. We have only two more boxes to sell."

"But I can arrange others, papa. I know how to find all the shells, and I can make the boxes. I shall always keep one as a pattern. We will go to Mother Crampton presently, and take her a finished box."

"Not to-day, dearest. I am too ill to leave the house."

"Then I shall have time to complete a second this afternoon."

The invalid sighed deeply, and his daughter left him for a while to put the rooms in order. Then she sat down by his side and arranged the shells, chatting about indifferent things, and trying her best to cheer him. At the same time, she felt a dull pain oppressing her, when she pictured to herself her father depending on her efforts for support. When she was shut into her tiny room at night, she wept bitterly. So soon as her tears were spent, she kneeled in prayer, and told out all her fears and hopes to her Father in Heaven, until she was quite calm and trustful again. "Why should I doubt God?" she asked herself. "He fed his people in the wilderness, and He has fed us many times."

Mr. Newton was less depressed next morning. "I am not so weak in body, Annie," he said, when she asked him how he had passed the night, "and my faith in God burns more brightly."

"I am so very, very glad, papa!"

"I wish you to carry two boxes to Mother Crampton this morning. Did you finish a third yesterday?"

"Not quite, but very nearly; it is far enough advanced to serve as a pattern."

Annie left the house just as Dick entered with his bundle. "That's my new boy, Miss," called the spinster from the shop.

The young girl bent her head to Dick, but did not speak. She walked quickly to Mother Crampton's, for she longed to tell her best friend about her father. She met with the heartfelt sympathy she so much needed; and at the same time, she was braced up to endure her trouble. It is a good thing you are old enough to help your father," said the dame; "there is mercy in that. Cheer up, deary; your invalid will grow reconciled to his blindness as time goes on. God gives more of Himself when he takes away outside props. He's been thinking of you already. I sold a box of shells last evening, and I have an order for one more at ten shillings and two more at a guinea each. The gentleman who requires them wants you to have them ready in a month as they are for birthday presents."

Annie felt greatly comforted and at last grew cheerful, for she was encouraged to depend on her own exertions and to have faith in God; added to this, the order for the three boxes would bring in enough money for several weeks' food and lodging. By degrees she and Mother Crampton conversed on other topics and Tom was not forgotten among them.

"I know that I shall find he's been more sinned against than sinning," remarked the dame. "I don't mean that he ought to have broken God's day; but I'm sure Dick Potter has been his worst enemy and led him into evil."

"Miss Pringle has a new boy," said Annie; "I saw him just now; but he has not a pleasant face."

"She has soon found a successor to Tom, then. I am very partial to that lad, and am glad that he is going to live opposite, and with such good people as Mr. and Mrs. Jones."

"I suppose you managed to secure the situation for him? You are always lending a helping hand, Mother Crampton. I am not the only one who has to thank you for kindnesses. Now, I am going back to persuade papa to take a walk with me, and I intend to be very bright and not allow myself to think how desolate I shall feel when I have to pick up shells alone, and realize that papa will never accompany me again."

"Be a brave little maiden, even if sad thoughts force themselves on you. Should Tom Gillies turn out as well as I expect he will, I'm sure he will be glad to help you; and I'm quite sure Mr. Jones will grant him an occasional half-holiday for the purpose.

"That is a famous idea," said Annie. "Mrs. Jones has always been very kind to me, and I shall not mind asking a favor of her."

In five minutes Annie was at home and standing by the invalid's side. "Capital news, papa," she said; then, noticing the traces of tears, she continued, in an anxious tone, "you have been crying, father; oh, do not, please, do not fret! I have an order for three more boxes. Now, come out for a walk—the air will refresh you," and she put his hat on and led him gently to the door and down the stairs.

Miss Pringle brushed past them in the passage. Mr. Newton drew back. "Did I hurt you," he asked. "I am quite blind now."

"No—nothing to speak of," she replied, hastily.

They walked slowly down the narrow pathway from the top of the cliff to the sands, Annie going first and holding her father's hand.

"How nicely you manage, papa," she said, "and how beautiful the air is; already you are better. We will sit down, while I tell you how every point looks, and which part is in the shadow." She prattled on until Mr. Newton was beguiled into asking questions, and forgot himself and his sorrow for awhile.

They remained out for more than an hour before he expressed a wish to return. Their simple dinner over, Annie arranged her shells. She was thus employed when a step was heard on the stairs, and Miss Pringle tapped at the door. A visit from her never boded any good, but generally heralded some unpleasantness.

"I came to say, I'm sorry you've gone blind, Mr. Newton," she began. "I'm sorry for two reasons: one for yourself, and the other because I'm obliged to give you notice, that if my rent isn't paid regularly, I can't keep you. I don't know how you'll live now, and I'm too poor to let my rooms for nothing. I thought it was better to speak plainly and come to some understanding."

Mr. Newton looked very much pained.

"If I fail in paying my rent, you may complain," he said; "but I think it would have been better for you to have waited until such was the case. My daughter can fit up the boxes of shells almost as well as I can, and we have several orders to execute. More I cannot say."

Annie's face flushed crimson, and she felt inclined to answer, "You cruel, unkind woman, how dare you behave thus?" but she restrained herself, and only replied, "I shall manage the rent, Miss Pringle; you may trust me."

"Very well, miss, that's enough; but I must be just to myself and look after my own interests, for I'm a lone woman," and the spinster left the room.

"Never mind her, papa!" exclaimed Annie, "we shall be as well off as before; and I know God will take care of us. I only wish we could change our lodging."

"Better not, child; we know all the disagreeables we have to put up with here."

"Miss Pringle is not a happy woman, and she is really very hard by nature, I do believe. How unkindly she behaves to her boys! I wonder if the new one she has now is the Dick Potter that Mother Crampton says has done so much harm, and been such a bad friend to Tom Gillies."

"As if there were not two boys of the same name at Dixtown."

"Still, papa, it is odd that he happens to be called Dick," persisted Annie.

Mr. Newton smiled at his daughter, and the conversation ended here.

CHAPTER XIII.

TOM'S FIRST WAGES.

AT the close of Dick's first week with Miss Pringle he had won a high place in her opinion; but not so with Annie or her father, who were duly informed by Mother Crampton of the cowardly part he had acted towards Tom.

Mr. Newton ventured to tell Miss Pringle she had done wrong when she engaged Dick, which made her extremely angry, and very insolent to her lodger, so sure was she that she had found a treasure.

Dick had to gain an end, and was resolved to get possession of the money he had seen counted almost every night since he came to live with Miss Pringle; but his chance of appropriating it seemed very remote, for the spinster kept her door so carefully locked. He heard her enlarge on her poverty, and knew her words were false; and he began to class her with himself, and to think he had a right to deceive her, as she in her turn was deceiving others; so he stole her fruit and sweets, and managed to thieve them so cleverly that she was not aware of the fact. If he exceeded his usual number of drops he put more flour into the bottles, and gave short measure to the children who came to the shop to spend their halfpennies; and he never carried apples out without taking several of the best, nor sold peaches without adding something to the price his mistress asked.

It was on the first Sunday afternoon which Tom spent in Mr. Jones' service that he met Dick; but before we describe the interview we here must tell how Tom prospered.

His holiday was a happy one, and he entered on his new situation with a light and glad heart. Mr. Jones received him kindly, and so did his wife. He passed his days thus:—He rose before five o'clock, and so soon as he was dressed he groomed and harnessed the old horse Tippler; then he accompanied his master to the garden and helped him to cut fresh vegetables and gather fruit. By half-past six they were back again, in order to be ready to drive on the machines down to the sea. Later on, Tom returned to the shop, which he cleaned out, or carried the vegetables round. In the evening he took the children on the sands. Willy, the eldest, was five, and he and Tom soon became fast friends. He was carrying him when he met

Dick; his master and mistress were sitting on a rock with the baby a little distance off. Tom did not see his former friend approaching, but when he heard the voice he knew so well, he turned abruptly away. Dick was not to be shaken off easily. "Don't turn away, Tom, like that," he whined; "think how many years we've been friends."

"But we ain't friends now, and some day I mean to tell Miss Pringle the whole truth."

Dick would like to have knocked Tom down, but such behavior, would, he knew, damage his cause, so he only whimpered, "Don't be hard on me; I'm sure you've got nothing to complain of; and getting a something every week, and I nothing; why I really did you a good turn."

"But you didn't mean to. If Mother Crampton hadn't helped me I might have gone my own way to the bad."

"Well, anyhow, you've tumbled on your legs, Tom, so do be friends. You'll come and see me sometimes, and I'll try to run in and look at you. I'm very lonely, and we used to be so fond of one another."

"Master allows no visitors, and I know Miss Pringle doesn't; and I'm very busy from morning till night; there's plenty for me to do," replied Tom; "we shall meet out sometimes."

"You're a lucky fellow to fall in with such nice people," replied Dick, "and yet, on the whole, Miss Pringle doesn't behave badly to me. I went to church with her this morning. I suppose she's not a rich woman, Tom?"

"No, she can't be, or she wouldn't be always saying she was poor; but she does a fair business, and, I'm sure, allows nothing to be wasted. I suppose her profits ain't large."

"Tom!" called his master at this moment, "we're moving."

The lad responded to the call with a hasty "good-bye," to his former companion.

"I hate him," snarled Dick, walking slowly away in the opposite direction.

That evening Tom went to see Mother Crampton, who was unwell. He heard from her about Mr. Newton's blindness, and determined to try and help Annie, with his master's permission, to find the shells she needed for her boxes. They spoke of Dick, and the old lady warned him against keeping up any acquaintances with his former companion.

"I never mean to again," said Tom, with great self-assurance. "I'm not to be caught so easily as I used to be."

"Don't be too positive," answered the dame; and then she added so many kind and loving words about God being the only refuge from temptation, and the need of getting daily

strength for daily need, by prayer, that Tom's
self-assurance vanished, and he told her about
killing grandmother's cat, and that he intended
to buy a new kitten for her, which was to have
a red collar.

"But you must tell your grandmother why
you give her the present."

"That's just what I expected you would say;
but it will be hard work."

"Not so hard as losing a cat. I'm indeed
grieved for your poor grandmother; lone people
can't help loving dumb creatures very much."

"But I did not mean to kill Tabby."

"Perhaps not; but you meant to do something
to pay off old scores, according to your own
confession. What else have you done wrong in,
Tom?"

"I stole a peach from Miss Pringle, and a
good many apples, and let Dick in two nights. I
do so wish I'd never done any of these wicked
things; for now I know better, I seem to have
tied knots in all directions, and I can't tell
whenever they'll be untied. If I hadn't them to
weigh me down, how thankful I should be."

"It's not too late to mend. You may untie the
most difficult knots if you will, by casting all
your care on God, and asking that His Spirit
may teach you: tell grandmother the whole
truth when you give her a new pet, and wait for
an opportunity of helping Miss Pringle, and

then say boldly to her why you wish to render her some service."

"Even tell her about Dick Potter?"

"Yes, even that when the right time comes."

Tom thought for a few moments ere he answered. "I really will conquer myself in the way you've advised, Mother Crampton. I'll go on praying."

"Then in the end you will conquer, so I'm not afraid. But I should be very sad if I felt you were going to try and reform yourself in your own strength."

"Thank you for all you've said," remarked Tom, when they had talked in the same strain for another half hour. "You look tired, so I'll be off. I shall run up to the Castle and then home."

Tom found two friends on the Castle Hill, Mr. Newton and his daughter. As they were sitting on one of the wooden benches, he ventured to approach them.

"Here is Tom Gillies," said Annie to her father.

"Ask him to come and tell me how he is getting on."

Tom took the seat next to Mr. Newton, and related the history of himself in his bluff, honest way; he also ventured to ask in conclusion, "May I do any thing for you, sir? I ain't got much time to spare; but while the

mornings are so light, I can be up first thing—
three o'clock isn't too soon for me."

Mr. Newton was touched. "I thank you,
Tom," he answered. "If my daughter goes to
pick up shells, you will be very useful; but I
think I must ask your master to grant you a
half-holiday."

"I'm sure he will!" exclaimed the boy. "I
shall be proud to help Miss Annie. I'll work off
hours for master, to make up."

"You're a kind-hearted lad," said Mr.
Newton, adding, with a deep sigh, "I am quite
blind now, and that makes me so helpless about
the shells. It's hard work, but there is a good
God over us all; He will care for me and my
child."

Annie's eyes filled. "Don't think of me,
father," she said, with an effort to be cheerful;
"Remember I am very clever, and Mother
Crampton manages to sell the boxes as quickly
as I can fill them."

"Bless you, my little daughter," said her
father, tenderly. "Tom," he added, earnestly,
"Serve God while you are young, and while
you have life and health. If I had not found rest
in believing, I do not know how I should have
endured my affliction. Now, Annie, let us be
moving."

Tom accompanied his friends down the
Castle Hill, and then went directly home.

The days passed smoothly along, until the end of the first month, when Mr. Jones paid Tom his first wages. The boy felt very rich; twelve shillings seemed an inexhaustible mine of wealth. He had laid it out many times before he actually spent it. First, he agreed to give two shillings for a kitten which had one of the finest tails ever seen, and two shillings for a new red collar. Then he had to purchase presents for Sally and his younger brothers and sisters.

"I wish I could manage to get a holiday from Saturday until Sunday night, or Monday morning first thing," thought Tom. "I'd sooner pay a shilling to get back, if Harry or Will ain't coming over. It's a deal of money, but I want to settle up with grandmother, besides the kitten and collar will be waiting. I'll ask master if I may go, and tell him I shan't want a holiday in six months' time, if I may have one on Saturday."

On Wednesday morning Tom preferred his request, as he and Mr. Jones drove to the market garden. He had carried his wages over to mother Crampton on the previous evening, and asked her to keep his money until he knew whether he could be spared on Saturday.

"Please, sir, I'm going to ask you a great favor. May I go home on Saturday until Sunday night or Monday morning?"

"What! Home-sick, Tom?"

"No, sir—not exactly."

"Then I suppose you want to take your first earnings to your mother. But no, it can't be that either when Mrs. Gillies is so often here. Well what is it?"

"It's a great secret, sir, between me and Mother Crampton; but I'll tell you if you promise to keep it."

"Yes, I will promise."

"I've seen a beautiful cat that I've said I'll buy for grandmother and I've ordered a red collar and I want to take it to her."

"Right, boy. You're good to remember the aged. Yes, you may go."

Tom thought for the first moment that he would not undeceive his master; then he felt that if he left Mr. Jones in ignorance of the truth he would be more troubled than if he told him everything—why he bought the kitten and why he wished to see his grandmother. His anxiety to untie old knots and to tie no new ones made him stammer out, "I don't deserve to be praised, sir, for I wronged grandmother; only I didn't mean to do what I did," and here he stopped and looked so uncomfortable that Mr. Jones said by way of encouragement—

"I should like to hear your story, Tom, if you can trust me. I've had troubles and temptations in my time, so perhaps I can help you."

Mr. Jones was as simple and true in his religious belief as in his dealings with men. He tried to be a Christian at all times; therefore he was in a position to be a wise and efficient help to Tom at this stage of his life's history. So the lad spoke openly to his master about the past nor did he conceal the struggle he had with himself before he resolved to confess his wrong-doing to grandmother when he gave her the kitten.

"You'd but half do your work if you left your grandmother in ignorance of the reason why you gave her a new cat. You shall have a holiday, and I'll lend you that nice covered basket of mine to carry the kitten in. I say, go on and prosper. You shall leave on Saturday afternoon and return on Monday; and if your brother's boat isn't coming, why I'll go shares in hiring one to bring you back."

"Oh thank you—thank you, sir. Now I am indeed happy. If only grandmother isn't very angry and will forgive me I shall be the jolliest fellow living."

"You must bear the old lady's anger, my boy; remember you deserve it. You took her child when you killed her Tabby, and it's to be expected that she'll feel indignant when she learns the truth. However, there's one cure— that is in prayer. Pray without ceasing that all may be well and that her heart may be softened toward you."

Tom was busy that week making his purchases. A third of this month's wages were consumed by grandmother's present. The Bible he bought for himself cost one shilling and sixpence; a yard of ribbon for Sally, and the promised copy of "Come to Jesus" took another shilling and penny; two shillings he reserved for his mother, who undertook to wash and mend his clothes at the rate of sixpence a-week; ten pennies were devoted to five boxes of toys for his younger brothers and sisters; and the balance that remained he handed back to Mother Crampton.

Tom saw his brother Will on Friday, who said he would be in Dixtown on the morrow and expected to leave the pier at four o'clock in the afternoon for Norton Island, and that he was obliged to come in again on Monday at six o'clock; so Tom's difficulties in this respect were removed and, in fact, all seemed to prosper for his proposed excursion.

Mrs. Gillies crossed with her sons on Saturday. The basket and parcel Tom carried gave rise to many questions and he had to acknowledge that he had been laying out some of his month's wages in presents.

"I hope you've not been spending your money foolishly," said his mother.

"No, not foolishly," answered Tom. "I wanted to buy these things; and from this time I mean to save."

Mrs. Gillies did not reprove Tom further. She had received a good character of him from Mrs. Jones; and as he handed her two shillings she merely added a few general remarks on the duty of being economical.

Tom, as may be supposed, had a hearty welcome at home. His young brothers and sisters crowded round him, and were so delighted with their presents that he felt quite a hero among them. Of course they wanted to know what the basket contained; and when Tom showed the kitten, the young ones clapped their hands with delight. The kitten seemed in no wise frightened at so many eyes peeping into her basket; she shook herself, and stepped from it quite quietly to lap some milk out of a saucer.

"Is it to stay here, Tom?" questioned one of his little sisters.

"No; it's for grandmother," he answered.

"Shall I go with you when you take it to her?" asked Sally.

"I'd rather go alone," he replied.

Directly after tea Tom started off, basket in hand. It was nearly seven o'clock when he reached grandmother's cottage; and as September was far advanced the evenings were beginning to draw in. Still there was light enough to see kitty, and Tom thought it was better to get over his interview at once rather than wait until the following day. He tapped softly at the door. Grandmother opened it and started back.

"You, Tom!" she said. "Ay, I remember they told me you were coming. I'm glad to hear a better account of you. Step in."

Grandmother had only once before spoken as civilly to Tom, and he felt very thankful that she was so inclined to be pleasant. He had carried out his master's and Mother Crampton's advice, and there seemed an answer to his prayers at the first starting.

"I'm getting on nicely," he answered sitting on a wooden stool close to grandmother, and clearing his throat which felt very husky. "And, you know, I have wages now; so I've spent part of my first month's money in buying you a present."

"Bought me a present! It's something quite new for me to have one; they're rare things, Tom."

And again granny spoke kindly.

The boy opened his basket, and, lifting the kitten out, placed her gently in the old woman's lap. Kitty, as if she knew what would please her new mistress best, curled herself round and lay still, purring and moving her tail gently up and down.

"What a beauty!" exclaimed grandmother. "Is this for me, Tom? It's handsomer than Tabby, I declare. Oh, how happy you've made me! And I don't deserve it, for I've been so unkind to you."

"Don't say that, grandmother; it's I who have been unkind to you. But I didn't mean it; I really didn't mean to kill your Tabby."

"Then you killed her after all?"

"Yes, grandmother; but this is how it was. You must listen while I tell you everything." And Tom gave a full description of how it all happened; that he was very angry when his grandmother declared she would tell tales of him and get him punished, and that seeing Tabby suggested the wicked thought, that if he were thrashed he would be thrashed for something. "And yet I hardly know what I wanted, grandmother," he added, "for I'm sure I didn't want Tabby to go mad or be killed, but I think I hoped something would come about that would pain you, because you were so cross with me. I've been so miserable ever since. Oh, do say you forgive me; please do."

"Forgive you, Tom! Yes, that I will; but I need your forgiveness as much as you need mine. It was cruel of you to treat Tabby as you did, but I'd no business to be so hard upon you.

I know I'm a cross-grained old woman, but I'll try and turn over a new leaf. To think of your spending your money on a new cat and buying such a smart collar too. I'm so pleased; and what's more, I hope I've learnt a lesson from you that will do me good as long as I live."

Tom did not leave his grandmother until after eight. He told her many things connected with his new life, and a great deal about Mr. Newton and his daughter. When they parted, she kissed him, and said "Never let us speak of the past again, and let no one know who killed Tabby. Tell your father that we mean to be good friends for the future. Come and see me tomorrow, and hear how my new Tabby—for she shall have the same name as my old pet— likes her quarters."

"I'll come," answered Tom. "I'm going to the service in the afternoon, for notice was given to the children at school this morning that a friend of Mr. Pender's would preach. Will you come too, grandmother?"

"I've never been yet."

"The more reason you should begin. Mr. Jones is very particular how I spend my Sunday and Mother Crampton says we ought to keep God's day holy. I like going to church twice now; I've only missed one evening since I've been at my new situation, and that was when Mother Crampton was ill."

"I tell you what I'll do. If you come and fetch me, I'll go with you to the schoolroom to-morrow. I must lock Tabby in, as she's strange here," said granny.

"I'll come in good time for the service," answered Tom as he left the cottage.

Sunday morning rose without a cloud. Tom was up early and bathed. Afterwards he took the little ones for a walk, and read to them out of his new Bible. Dinner was at twelve, and at half-past two the bell began to ring for the afternoon service. Most of the cottagers went to the schoolroom for Mr. Pender told his men he hoped they would all attend; so some went out of curiosity, others to please their master, and a few because they loved to hear about their Saviour.

"Tom, I shan't forget what I've heard in a hurry," said grandmother as they walked home after the service. "It's an easy text to remember—'Turn ye, turn ye, why will ye die? And he looks close on death himself. What a deal I've got to learn, according to him. I'm wrong altogether."

"The gentleman said in grander words just what Mother Crampton told me," answered Tom, "that every one who won't come to Christ will die in their sins. Oh, grandmother, I've been trying so hard to believe and learn of Jesus in the last few weeks—"

"And I'll try too, Tom. You must know there was a time in my life when my heart was softer, but it's grown hard with years and living alone, and for a long time I've given up praying to God to make it soft again; but now I'll begin to pray."

Tom accompanied his grandmother home to see how kitty had conducted herself in their absence, and she asked him to stay to tea.

"I'd like to," he replied, "only Sally will be disappointed if I don't go home."

"Let her come here; I shall like to have her."

Tom went to fetch his sister. Sally was greatly surprised when he gave his invitation, but very glad to accept it.

After a cozy tea drinking, grandmother asked Tom to read her a chapter from the Bible. He complied with her request and later on read to her from "Come to Jesus;" first about tying and untying knots, and then the words addressed to the aged. When he ended granny was weeping. "It means me," she sobbed. "I've not heeded the warnings God has given me. I've got white hair and wrinkled features, and I've not a moment to lose for I'm an old woman; but, Tom, I'll come to Jesus at once, for He also can save."

"I've untied a big knot since yesterday," thought Tom, ere he fell into a sound sleep and dreamed sweet dreams. But no sleep and no bright dreams came to Miss Pringle on that Sunday night, nor to Mr. Newton nor his daughter Annie. The reason why we must reserve for another chapter.

CHAPTER XIV.

THE ACCIDENT.

DICK was no nearer the wished-for money on that Saturday afternoon when Tom went home, nor did he see any chance of clutching the prize. He was growing weary of controlling himself, and vexed and annoyed that his former friend avoided him; for when they met, Tom passed on with a few civil words of greeting, but refused to make an appointment to walk out.

Miss Pringle had not been feeling quite so well of late—not that much ailed her—but she was very tired after her day's work and extremely cross. She was sensible, too, that it cost her a greater effort than was usual to lift her gold up and down from the cupboard shelf, and determined to change some of her hardly-earned sovereigns into crisp bank-notes.

On the Sunday night which brought such pleasant dreams to Tom, she retired to her room at the usual hour. Dick did not watch his mistress count her money quite so regularly as in the first fortnight, for he knew the process so well. He was falling asleep without having first looked through the keyhole, and was startled by hearing a loud crash overhead. He jumped up and listened, for he fancied it was followed by a low moan. Mr. Newton and his daughter Annie, who were about to separate for the night, heard the noise too, and Annie rushed to the door and opened it, when she heard the words, "Help me."

"Can you let me in?" she asked.

"No; I'm too much hurt," groaned Miss Pringle, with great difficulty.

"We must force the door," said Mr. Newton. "Can you see through the keyhole, Annie?"

"Yes, quite well. Miss Pringle is lying on the floor half in her cupboard. She must have fallen."

"You had better call Dick."

Just at this moment the boy joined them, but the united efforts of the three made no impression on the door, and Dick was sent to fetch a locksmith.

At last admittance was gained. A stool with a broken leg revealed how the accident had happened.

Miss Pringle was quite unconscious. With the help of the locksmith, they placed her on her bed; for Mr. Newton's blindness prevented him from taking an active part.

"Now run for a doctor, Dick," said Annie. "The one who lives in the first house on the terrace is the nearest."

It was quite half-an-hour before the doctor came, during which time the young girl sat still and waited, not knowing what she ought to do.

Though Dick's face expressed great sorrow, he was secretly rejoicing over Miss Pringle's fall, hoping that it might in some way facilitate his wishes, and that he would gain possession of her gold.

"This is a sad business," said the doctor, after he had examined his patient. "I can scarcely tell the extent of the mischief, nor whether her arm and leg are broken or only sprained. I can do nothing until tomorrow morning, the limbs are swelling so rapidly. Has she a friend who can sit up with her? She must not be left."

"I do not think she has a single friend or relation in the world," replied Annie.

"Poor thing! She is to be pitied. I have heard she is very eccentric; but having lived so short a time in this neighborhood, I am but little acquainted with its inhabitants."

"I will remain with her," said Annie. "I hope in the morning she will be well enough to say what she wishes to be done; and her boy is here to take any message that is necessary."

"That is sufficient. You had better not attempt to move her without help. Give her some drops that I will send you at once. Her consciousness will soon return, I hope."

When the doctor left, he was accompanied by Dick. Then Annie took counsel of her father as to whether she should call in assistance from any of the neighbors.

"Better not, my dear," answered Mr. Newton. "Miss Pringle may turn on us, and say we must pay, as she gave no orders. You can manage with Dick to-night, and to-morrow morning the doctor must arrange, if she be too ill to be consulted."

So soon as Dick returned with the medicine, Annie persuaded her father to go to bed, knowing that any excitement or want of rest would be attended with bad after-consequences.

"Call me, Dick," she said, "if you notice any change. I shall not be long. I am going to see after papa."

"Now is my time," thought the boy. "If I can once get the box out of the cupboard and down stairs, I am safe. When missus comes to herself it will be too late. Now or never. I shall have time to get away from Dixtown, for she'll never say she's got money unless she's obliged; only I must be quick."

He assured himself that Miss Pringle was still unconscious ere he carried a chair into the cupboard, and lifted the bandbox on to the ground. He took out the wooden box, replaced the bandbox, and carried the chair back, leaving the cupboard door exactly as it was before.

"All right so far," he said to himself. "Three minutes more will finish my business."

Two candles were burning, so that there was light enough to see his way clearly. He took hold of the box with a firm grip, and was moving off with it, when Annie opened the door softly, and entered the room, while at the same moment Miss Pringle unclosed her eyes, gave a loud shriek, and moaned, "Oh, dear, oh, dear, what shall I do?"

Annie could not have explained why she appeared at this juncture, except that she had an uneasy feeling at leaving Dick alone with the spinster. Seeing him box in hand, she screamed out, "Papa, papa, Dick's stealing. Call out of the window for help."

Her sudden coming and appealing to her father, coupled with Miss Pringle's scream, made Dick loosen his hold of the box, which fell heavily; while the would-be thief pushed rudely past, rushed down stairs, and out of the back door, as Mr. Newton called "Help, help!"

"What's the matter?" asked Mr. Wilkins, who was smoking his pipe in front of his house. He and his wife had only just returned home from spending the day with friends, otherwise they would have known that something unusual had occurred next door.

"We want you and your wife here. Annie will open the door for you," said Mr. Newton.

Annie could not come at that moment, for she was by Miss Pringle's side. The sudden start she made when she screamed, had brought on intense pain, and she lay with closed eyes again.

"Papa, I must have help," cried Annie.

"Wilkins is waiting below," answered her father, sadly. He felt so much and almost bitterly his infirmity just then; it seemed to come before him in an appalling form; he was so helpless to render his child any assistance in her sore need.

In a few minutes Annie unfastened the front door, and admitted the good couple. Mrs. Wilkins had often rendered her assistance, and was ready to help any who were in distress. Her story was soon told.

"You go up and see what you can do," said Mr. Wilkins to his wife, when he had heard a few facts; "I'll search after Dick; if he's clean gone, he may go, as you've saved the property,

Miss Annie. There is no fear of his ever troubling Miss Pringle again."

So soon as Mrs. Wilkins entered the spinster's room, her first care was to put the box and its contents into a place of safety. The sides were somewhat damaged by the fall, the weight of the sovereigns having loosened the nails.

"This explains much to me," she said to Annie. "See, miss, the stocking is full of money. Miss Pringle has always spoken of her poverty, and now I understand the secret of her life. The love of getting gold has mastered her. It's very, very sad."

By the time that the wooden box was deposited in the cupboard, and the broken stool removed, Mr. Wilkins tapped at the door, and said, "I find no trace of Dick. He must have run away through the fields. I've fastened the kitchen door; and I'll go home. The boy is no loss; I've known him for many years, and I warned the missus here to beware when she engaged him, and told her plainly she'd made a mistake. Good night. You can call me if you want me."

Annie and Mrs. Wilkins conversed in whispers until Miss Pringle was so far restored as to be able to take the medicine prescribed by the doctor. "Now try and sleep," they said.

"Where am I? And what has happened?" asked Miss Pringle.

Annie answered in as few words as possible, and promised to be more explicit in the morning. The spinster closed her eyes wearily, and her nurses had the great satisfaction of seeing her fall into a quiet sleep.

The injuries which she had received were very severe. One leg was broken, and the right arm badly sprained. It would be many weeks, even months, before she would be able to knead her bread. She would have to lie still, and be waited upon.

By degrees Miss Pringle received a full account of what had transpired. When Annie told her how nearly Dick had stolen her gold, she literally shivered with terror, and could not be quieted until her treasure had been counted out before her, and she had assured herself that not one sovereign was missing.

She had many long hours of pain in the first days after her accident, but pain of mind as well as body. She was humbled and mortified when she realized that her secret was known, and that her lodgers and neighbors were aware she was a false woman, and her pretended poverty a lie intended to deceive them. Her precautions had miserably failed; her future was dark and gloomy; her dearly-cherished gold must decrease; and what was more terrible was that she might be unable to work again; and what then? Had she befriended Mr. Newton in his sore need? Had she ever helped anyone who was sick or in trouble? She moaned many times, as if in severe pain, when it was mental anguish that called forth the expression, and not the aching of hurt limbs.

Mrs. Wilkins was engaged for part of every day. She had no children to occupy her time, and was able to attend to her husband's wants and see to the invalid; but she could not undertake more. Miss Pringle felt her business must be left for the present—until she was well; but what if she were a cripple for life?

It was a week after the accident that Tom called to see the spinster. He did not come before, because he had been passing through a sharp conflict with himself. He had heard every particular of the trouble that had befallen her, and Dick's conduct, from Mother Crampton; for Annie had minutely described the circumstances to her old friend, and also added her own judgment in the matter. It was this:— When the young girl had time to think and wonder how Dick came to discover that Miss Pringle had a hoard of money, she remembered how easily she had seen through the keyhole. He must have arrived at the knowledge of her secret in the same manner. She ventured at last to ask Miss Pringle if she had any particular time for counting her money, and the spinster confessed that she had, and stated when it was.

"Now I understand all," said Annie to her. "Dick has watched you through the keyhole when you thought he was in bed."

This was by no means a pleasant conclusion to arrive at, so far as Miss Pringle was concerned; nevertheless, as we know, it was a correct one. When Annie told Mother Crampton, she agreed with her; and when Mother Crampton, in her turn, told Tom, it flashed into his mind that it was his fault in the first instance, for had he not housed Dick for two nights? Certainly he must have mastered the secret then, hence his behavior to himself, and his eagerness to serve Miss Pringle. Tom saw it all so plainly that he wondered he had been so blind before. First he felt very angry that Dick had gained his end so ignobly; then his anger turned into thankfulness that Dick had been prevented from taking the money; and in the end one idea fixed itself, which was, that he ought to offer his services to his former mistress. This decision brought on the sharp battle with himself, for he was very happy in his new situation, and dreaded leaving his very kind master.

First he consulted Mother Crampton, who encouraged him to go forward. She heartily pitied Miss Pringle, in spite of her many faults, and thought that even if Tom sacrificed his present position, his character would be matured by the voluntary surrender of his own wishes, because of his anxiety to be of service to one whom he thought he had wronged. She bade him speak to Mr. Jones, and come to no decision hastily.

Mr. Jones refused to settle the question by expressing a strong opinion either way. He advised Tom to ask God to help him to do right, and added, "So far as I am concerned, I shall be sorry to lose you, but I do not feel it right to throw any obstacle in the way of your carrying out what you believe to be the best."

So Tom paused for one week before he called on Miss Pringle, who was greatly surprised to hear from Mrs. Wilkins that Tom Gillies desired to see her. She had never quite forgiven his sending for his clothes, and was inclined not to receive him, for she could not be persuaded to believe, all at once, that Dick was such a wicked boy, even though she had good reasons for doubting anything that the latter had either said or done. Mrs. Wilkins liked Tom, and urged the spinster to allow him to have his way. "He seems so anxious for a quiet chat with you, that I think you mustn't refuse him," she pleaded. So he was invited to walk up.

When Tom found himself alone with his old mistress, he inquired after her health, and expressed his sorrow that so sad an accident had befallen her, but with such evident sympathy that Miss Pringle was softened towards him; and she opened the subject of the conversation which was uppermost in Tom's mind by asking him why he left her without giving any notice.

Tom asked her to listen to his story, which she did without once interrupting him. "And now," he said, in conclusion, "I've a good character from Mr. Jones, and I've come to say that if you'll take me back, I am ready to serve you again. I don't think you'll have cause to be sorry, for I really mean to help you; and though I'm very happy with Mr. Jones, and getting a salary, yet, if you'll give me only half what I get now I think I could manage. I mustn't expect them at home to buy me clothes after having had three shillings a week, for then mother would blame me. I owe you something, Miss Pringle, for behaving to you as I did, and for letting Dick into your house. Probably he could never have known that you had money, but for me, nor have tempted me to go to Lockstone, and behave as he did. Please forgive me; and to show you forgive me, let me be your boy again. There's another change come over me, which makes me think I shall

do better than before. I tell God all my troubles
and pleasures, and ask, in Christ's name, that
His Spirit may teach me what is right, and I've
found a deal of difference. I just try to untie as
many knots of sin as I can, and I try to tie no
fresh ones; but not in my own strength, I pray."

Tom did not know how thoroughly he
conquered Miss Pringle by the simple
straightforward way in which he told his story,
and detailed his difficulties, and shortcomings,
for she merely replied, "I forgive you, Tom,
and thank you for your offer; let me have until
to-morrow to decide."

Tom rose to go, but still lingered, for he had a
few more words to add, which he found rather
difficult to bring out. "Please, Miss Pringle,
you won't be offended if I speak to you about
something else," he summoned up courage to
stammer out at last.

"No, Tom, you may say what you have to say
freely."

"It's only this: When I was with you, I didn't
feel your religion was quite real. Don't please,
be offended. You said a great deal, and you
made me read the commandments to you, and
you went to church, and all that; but at home
you were hard, and had no kind words for me;
and when I talked to Mother Crampton, I felt
there was something so real in all she said, and
it was just the same with my new master, Mr.

Jones. I found him a Christian from morning until night; and I'm trying hard to learn that sort of religion, and I'm happier for it; and I want you to do the same. I've brought you a little book that's helped me; it has the words about tying and untying knots in it that first made me think, and I've turned down the page for you. I hope you ain't offended at my speaking."

"No, Tom," Miss Pringle answered again.

The boy stepped forward, and put the book into her hand, and saying, "Good-bye; I shall call to-morrow for your answer," left the room, but not the house, for Annie called him in to see her father; and when he had told them what he had done, they hoped very much that Miss Pringle would accept his offer.

"She is softened already by her misfortune," said Annie. "She even told me yesterday that she had sinned in loving her money so much. Why, Tom, she has more than two hundred sovereigns! I counted them out before her. I wish she would send them to the bank."

"Do not be so impatient, Annie," answered Mr. Newton. "Miss Pringle has much to learn. I had rather that she acted after mature thought, than in such a great hurry."

When Tom closed the door on his old mistress, she fell into a long reverie. She glanced back over many years of her life, and felt the retrospect was not a pleasant one. She had lived to make money, and cut herself off from all that brings true joy in life, merely to accumulate gold. Her one thought had been to gather and to keep. And now she was lying helpless, and that which had been her idol must go to keep her from starving. Tom's words about her professions of religion came with startling truth. She had kept up a sort of sham piety all her life; she had served God formally, but had not given her heart to Him, but to her money. She grew so restless and uneasy at last, that Annie, who came in, as was her wont, several times during the day, noticed how flushed she was, and asked, "Are you suffering much pain?"

"No, Miss Annie," she replied; "I am not suffering bodily in pain, but my heart aches so. I've made a great mistake. I've lived for money, and I can't bear to think of it."

Annie left the room, and returned in a few minutes, bringing her Bible with her. She chose several passages from the Gospels, which she thought best suited to Miss Pringle's state of mind, and she read on until she found that the sacred word brought some degree of peace and rest. Before she went back to her shells she ventured to say, "Pray, Miss Pringle; God will hear the prayer of the penitent. There is joy in heaven over the repentant sinner."

The spinster could not sleep that night, so busy was she with herself. The next morning she sent for Mr. Newton, and told him she had made up her mind to take Tom Gillies back to carry on her business. She also asked him if he would be good enough to go to the bank and deposit her money, and concluded by begging him to forgive her unkindness and selfishness.

"I did not know what it was to be helpless when I spoke so cruelly to you," she said; "but God is teaching me. I believe being laid by will do me good, but it's early days yet for me to say this."

Tom came at noon, and was with Miss Pringle for more than one hour. The result of the interview was that he engaged to take up his quarters under the staircase on the following day, at the same salary he received from Mr. Jones. Neither Miss Pringle nor he ever spoke of that conversation to a third party, but it was quite evident that Tom and his mistress had been deeply moved, for there were traces of tears in their eyes, and from this time quite another tie existed between them, Tom was treated more like a son than an errand-boy.

CHAPTER XV.

TWO YEARS LATER.

TWO years later Dixtown appeared just the same to a casual observer as on the day when we closed our last chapter. The sun shone as brightly, the birds sang as gaily, the myrtles, fuchsias, and fig-trees flourished as luxuriantly, and the bay looked as placid. Nevertheless, some changes had taken place: one old-established shop had ceased to be; one new shop had been opened; and some of the inhabitants had been laid in their last resting-place in the pretty cemetery on the hill-side.

Mother Crampton was one of these; she had finished her course with joy, and had passed up quietly and trustfully, depending on no righteousness of her own, but on the finished work of her Saviour, to the home prepared for her, among the mansions of the blest. She had no long illness; she worked to within a week of her decease, when she was compelled to take to her bed. She was tended by loving ones to whom she had so often ministered;—Annie, Tom, Mrs. Jones, ay, even Miss Pringle on her crutches, were with her, each vying with the other in giving her some token of their respect and love. After her death her home passed into the hands of a respectable fisherman, but the shop was abandoned, for his wife had too large a family of children to be able to attend to it. This necessitated Annie's finding another means of disposing of her boxes, and in her distress Miss Pringle helped her.

The spinster's recovery had been tedious, and no perfect cure was effected: she would never be able to walk again without her crutches. The illness had borne ripe fruit; it had softened the hard lines in her character. The change came very gradually, there was so much leaven to purge out; but the heart of stone can be turned to flesh when under the sanctifying influence of true religion; and Miss Pringle's former service of God had merged into vital Christianity.

Tom soon mastered the baking business in all its details; he lost no old customers, but gained may new ones, for the Dixtown people said that his bread was, if anything, superior to Miss Pringle's; and as the story of her affliction, and her generous behavior spread, several came to the shop by way of encouragement. When Tom

became so essential to the spinster, she offered
to give notice to her lodgers to find new
apartments, as the only way of procuring him a
more comfortable bedroom; the lad refused to
accept a change on these terms, for he enjoyed
spending part of every evening with Mr.
Newton and his daughter; they were too good
friends of his to be thus summarily dismissed.
But after Mother Crampton died, and Annie's
difficulties about disposing of her boxes arose,
Tom went to his mistress and suggested that
she should rent the adjoining cottage, and
install her lodgers in it.

Miss Pringle offered no objection; Annie had
been so good to her that she was glad to have it
in her power to make some return. She not only
took the cottage, but spent a little money in
making necessary alterations, which is the best
proof we can urge of the great change that had
taken place in her character.

The first year of Annie's attempt at shop-
keeping had just closed. It had been a profitable
one; in addition to her boxes she sold
anemones, sea-weed, fossils, shells, and ferns.
She and Tom had studied natural history with
Mr. Newton, until they learned to search after,
and distinguish the rare specimens which
abounded everywhere on the beautiful coast.

Mr. Newton was in much better health, and
with renewed strength his eyesight was

partially restored; he was able to serve customers, prepare boxes, and even read a few pages of a large-printed book.

So soon as Annie and her father were established in their new quarters, Tom exchanged his hole under the staircase for the large room they had occupied, so that he, too, was materially benefited, but yet retained his best friends near at hand.

"Any prawns wanted. Prawns to sell," cried Mrs. Gillies, walking up the street one bright October morning, and entering Miss Pringle's shop. "Good day!" she said, on perceiving the spinster busily dusting her shelves. "Is Tom too busy to speak to me for a few moments?"

"O, no!" answered Miss Pringle, in a cheerful tone, for she could be bright now; could smile, and sometimes laugh heartily. "He's just taken the bread out of the oven."

Tom entered the shop at this moment. He was now in his seventeenth year, and had grown into a tall, handsome lad.

"I've a message from granny," said Mrs. Gillies. "She wants to see you if you can come over on Tuesday. She's not been well the last few days. I wish she'd give up her cottage and live with us. She's too old to be left, and there's room now that Harry and Will are gone, and Sally's so soon to be married. Persuade her to come."

"Yes, I will, mother. Isn't she a happy old woman now? I like to think of her."

"Yes, that she is, and it's your doing, Tom," answered his mother. "You've done a great deal, my boy, for many of us," she added emphatically.

"It was Miss Annie's book that made me think first," said Tom; "but after all, we must thank God."

"Yes," replied Mrs. Gillies. "I, for my part, am glad things have changed with us. I do thank God for it, and I'm sure your father does. I hope I shall live to see all my children Christians before I die. I feel plenty on my conscience sometimes, Miss Pringle, when I think of my past wickedness, and how often I've been a bad mother. I wish—oh, how I do wish—I'd loved God all my life."

"So do I; we've all a deal to grieve over," added the spinster.

"We're more ready to tie than untie knots," remarked Tom.

"But how blessed it is for us all to know God forgives us in Christ, and accepts our feeble efforts to live nobler and better lives," said Miss Pringle.

The conversation was interrupted here by the postman entering with a letter, which he gave to Tom. The boy started when he read it, and turned very pale. "It's from Dick, mother; he's sentenced to be transported for ten years, with hard labor."

"He's young enough to have such a sentence!" exclaimed Mrs. Gillies. "He's not nineteen, Tom."

"No, mother."

"It's very, very sad," remarked Miss Pringle. "Dick is associated with a great deal of sorrow and much joy. I feel sometimes as Jacob must have felt when the angel left him. 'Contented now upon my thigh to halt till life's short journey end.'"

"I wish—how I do wish—I could see him," said Tom. "It's too far to go—he's in London. Good-bye, mother, I must be off to my work."

But before Tom returned to the day's duties, he retired to his room to think. He was appalled at the news he had just received. Though he knew his former friend was running a downward course, this was too dreadful to realize.

From the moment that Dick fled through the fields on that night when Annie surprised him with Miss Pringle's wooden box, he had thrown off the mask he had assumed, and became thoroughly reckless. He was several times confined in the county prison for petty thefts; and when his father at last refused to admit him at home he joined a strolling party, and ultimately united himself to a band of desperate house-breakers, who made him their tool. Now that he was quitting his native land for so many years as a common felon, his thoughts reverted to his former companion, and he could not leave England without sending him a few words of farewell.

Tom read his letter again, and then fell on his knees and wept and prayed—not because he was better than Dick, but because through the mercy of God, he had been awakened to a sense of sin. He went about his work with a heavy heart, for he was haunted by the remembrance of Dick. He could neither read with, nor be taught by, Mr. Newton that evening—he could only speak of the contents of the letter he had received in the morning.

After he bade farewell for the night to Mr. Newton, he turned to Annie, and said, in a broken voice, "Miss Annie, Dick's letter has brought back all my past life, and how much I owe to you for giving me a helping hand. I never shall forget the Sunday when you gave me 'Come to Jesus,' and I read, 'Habit will fasten strong chains around you, which will be harder to burst asunder every day. While you wait, Satan works. He is busy tying knots. You are his prisoner, and he is making more and more secure the cords which bind you. Whenever you sin, he ties another knot.' Miss

Annie, thank you for showing me how Jesus is the only One who can untie those knots."

Lamplighter Rare Collector's Series

The Basket of Flowers. CHRISTOPH VON SCHMID
First written in the late seventeen hundreds, this book is the first in the **Lamplighter Collector's Series** which gave birth to Lamplighter Publishing. Come to the garden with the godly gardener, James, and his lovely daughter, Mary, and you will see why Elisabeth Elliot and Dr. Tedd Tripp so highly recommend this rare treasure.

Titus: A Comrade Of The Cross. F. M. KINGSLEY
In 1894 the publisher of this book gave a $1,000 reward to any person who could write a manuscript that would set a child's heart on fire for Jesus Christ. In six weeks, the demand was so great for this book that they printed 200,000 additional copies! You and your family will fall in love with the Savior as you read this masterpiece.

A Peep Behind The Scenes. O. F. WALTON
Behind most lives, there are masks that hide our hurts and fears. As you read, or more likely cry, through this delicate work, you will understand why there is so much joy in the presence of angels when one repents. Once you read it, you will know why two-and-a-half-million copies were printed in the 1800s.

Jessica's First Prayer. H. STRETTON
What does a coffee maker have in common with a barefoot little girl? You will want to read this classic over and over again to your children as they gain new insights into compassion and mercy as never before.

Stepping Heavenward. ELIZABETH PRENTISS
Recommended by Elisabeth Elliot, Kay Arthur, and Joni Eareckson Tada, this book is for women who are seeking an intimate walk with Christ. Written in 1850, this book will reach deeply into your heart and soul with fresh spiritual insights and honest answers to questions that most women and even men would love to have settled.

Joel: A Boy of Galilee. ANNIE FELLOWS JOHNSTON
If you read *Titus: A Comrade of the Cross* and loved it, let me introduce you to Joel. This is a story about a handicapped boy who has to make a decision whether to follow the healer of Nazareth or the traditions of the day. You will talk about this treasure for years.

Christie's Old Organ. O.F. WALTON
This is a child's story for all ages. Join a little boy named Christie and an old organ grinder as they search for the path that leads to heaven. This dramatic story has already led children to the saving knowledge of Jesus Christ. Be prepared to cry.

Jessica's Mother. H. STRETTON AND M. HAMBY
(sequel to Jessica's First Prayer)
Rewritten by Mark Hamby, this sequel will take you through the emotions of the greatest of all sacrifices. Embittered against God and anyone who bears the name of Christ, Jessica's mother is determined to take her daughter back regardless of the consequences. This is a story of human tragedy and divine love that will inspire families to take a second look at the real meaning of the gospel of Jesus Christ.

The Inheritance. CHRISTOPH VON SCHMID
This is another classic by the author of *The Basket of Flowers*. Seeking first the Kingdom of God and His righteousness will be a theme that parents and children will see through the eyes of a faithful grandson and his blind grandfather.

The Lamplighter. MARIA S. CUMMINS
Written in the 1800's when lamplighters lit the street lights of the village, this story will take you on a spiritual journey depicting godly character that will inspire and attract you to live your Christian life with a higher level of integrity and excellence. Mystery, suspense, and plenty of appealing examples of integrity and honor will grip the heart of anyone who reads this masterpiece.

The Hedge of Thorns. ANONYMOUS
Based on a true story about a little boy who will do almost anything to find out what is on the other side of a hedge of thorns. Enticed and frustrated, a child is about to learn why boundaries are a necessary part of God's plan for his life.

Mary Jones and Her Bible. ANONYMOUS
Another true story of a little girl whose strongest desire in life is to possess her very own Bible. Through hard work, determination, prayer, faith, and even a twenty-five mile walk, Mary Jones will do whatever it takes to obtain a copy of the Word of God. This true story will not only kindle a fire in children's hearts but give them a role model to follow that exemplifies hard work, faithfulness, and the reward of patient obedience.

The White Dove. CHRISTOPH VON SCHMID
This is another classic by the author of *The Basket of Flowers* that will once again lay a beautiful pattern of godliness for all to follow. Surrounded by knights and nobles, thieves and robbers, this story will take parent and child to the precipice of honor, nobility, sacrifice, and the meaning of true friendship. If you enjoyed *The Basket of Flowers*, you will not want to miss *The White Dove*.

Mothers of Famous Men. ARCHER WALLACE

Take a step back in time and visit with the great mothers of great men. Join Mrs. Washington, Mrs. Wesley, Mrs. Franklin, Mrs. Adams, Mrs. Lincoln, Mrs. Carnegie and many others and see what type of motherhood shaped such unusual greatness. You will enter their homes as well as their hearts, as you learn for the first time, portions of history rarely revealed. This is a book every parent and young person needs to read.

Clean Your Boots, Sir? ANONYMOUS

Finally, a book for boys that I would say equals *The Basket of Flowers*! In this captivating story you will meet a brave little boy who cares for his ailing father and two baby brothers. As a shoeshine boy, the little savings that he makes each day is just enough to meet their basic needs until a small act of honesty changes his life forever. Join the shoeshine boy as he introduces your children to integrity, honesty, faith, and sacrifice, in a way that they will never forget!

Melody, The Story of A Child. LAURA E. RICHARDS

An inspiring and beautifully written story that invites the reader to see life through the eyes of a most unusual child. Each chapter is filled with charming freshness as a blind child weaves her gift of "seeing" into the hearts of friend and foe alike. Themes: uncompromising love, discernment, childlike honesty, faith and forgiveness.

The Lost Ruby. CHRISTOPH VON SCHMID

Another classic that will teach children the important lesson of honesty regardless of the cost. Also included is one of Von Schmid's finest short stories, **The Lost Child**. This is a story of mystery and intrigue as the reader learns that God allows hardships for our good.

The Little Lamb. CHRISTOPH VON SCHMID

This story will teach our readers that all things do work together for good to them who love God. Parents and children will be filled with captivating suspense as they taste and see that the Lord is the God of the impossible.

True Stories of Great Americans for Young Americans. ANONYMOUS

Written for young readers, this edition of American history will inspire and reveal the character qualities and difficult circumstances that led these Americans to greatness. The seldom heard stories of George Washington, Robert E. Lee, Patrick Henry and many more will inspire and challenge young readers to value the past and guard the present as they themselves become agents of change for the future.

Boys of Grit Vol. 1 & 2. ARCHER WALLACE

Children and adults will be inspired when they read about boys who overcame great misfortunes, trials, and overwhelming circumstances to become great and godly men. When so many others saw only difficulties, they saw possibilities.

The Three Weavers. ANNIE FELLOWS JOHNSTON

Fathers and daughters will take a journey back to Camelot and learn the unforgettable lessons of virtue and vice.

The Stolen Child. CHRISTOPH VON SCHMID

Another Von Schmid classic that captures the beauty of God's creation as seen through the eyes of a child who lived in darkness most of his childhood. Lessons of responsibility and forgiveness are among the many virtues taught in this classic.

Always in His Keeping. ANONYMOUS

Based on a true story during the time of John Wesley, a brother and sister who are stolen as infants struggle to find their true identity and the faith to rest in a God who sometimes allows the righteous to suffer.

The Pillar of Fire. J.H. Ingraham

This is the most eloquently written, filled with the most illustrative accounts of the Prince of Tyre during his visit to Egypt over 3500 years ago. The author brings full color and inspiration to every page, while weaving his most suspenseful dramas in connection with the Scriptures. Truly, a fresh breath of literary air.

Rosa of Linden Castle. CHRISTOPH VON SCHMID

In this unique Von Schmid classic, a daughter's love for her condemned father will inspire children of all ages to see that though it was meant for evil, God always intends it for good.

Teddy's Button. AMY LEFEUVRE

Here's a story that will warm your heart, make you laugh, and above all, will help children to understand the spiritual battle that rages in their souls. Join Teddy as he demonstrates that even a child can enlist in God's army and carry the banner of love and victory high.

The Golden Thread. NORMAN MACLEOD

There was once a kingdom that dwelt near the treacherous Hemlock forest where an evil king and his followers dwelt. Citizens knew that only those who held the Golden Thread could wander past the boundaries of the kingdom and even then only those who held the thread by faith would be able to return.

Stick to the Raft. MRS. GEORGE GLADSTONE

This is a story that children will never forget. Young and old, will enjoy taking a journey with a poor young boy who is honored for his hard work and honesty. Just when things were looking up, misfortune which is really disguised as the providence of God, enters his life as he becomes the plot for mischief among jealous friends. Children and young adults will learn the important lessons that there is no fear in love and that forgiveness and truth are the greatest healers of all.

Stephen: A Soldier of the Cross. F.M. KINGSLEY

The long awaited sequel to Titus is finally here! Beginning in the deserts of Egypt, a blind sister and her powerful brother, find themselves the target of desert thieves. After hearing the reports of miracles in Jerusalem, they find themselves in the midst of the greatest, most life-changing event in history. But will it be too late for the blind girl? Readers will find themselves engulfed in this intense drama that unfolds at the foot of the cross.

Christie, the King's Servant. O.F. WALTON

In the sequel to Christies Old Organ, we find Christie pastoring a small parish in England, where a forgotten acquaintance steps back into his life. Here in this quaint village where fisherman take to their boats for a living, there is intense drama each time the clouds and winds begin to blow. Filled with delicate love and unusual hospitality, each reader will find it hard to take when Duncan's boat is found battered and empty days after the search has ended. Loss is never easy but this is one loss that our readers will never forget!

Probable Sons. AMY LEFEUVRE

Etched into the heart issues of unforgiveness and reconciliation, Probable Sons is a delightful book that will keep you smiling throughout. In a world of broken relationships, our little heroine Milly will help us tear away the layers of stubbornness and pride to provide a path that can help restore the injured from the most hurtful pain of the past. May the truths found in this little story find a resting place in many hearts that have strayed so far from home.

What is Her Name? REV. DR. EDERSHEIM

In the opening paragraph, the reader will begin to experience the skill with which the author of this story writes. Dr. Edersheim is truly a master of his craft. From the onset the reader will be drawn into the kind of mystery and intrigue that only a master of words can accomplish. Filled with mystery and intrigue, readers will find the providence of God woven throughout these pages. Join our little maiden and enjoy the innocence and purity that she models.

The Highland Chairman and Hans the Crucified.

The power of the first story in this book is in the influence that it carries, long after it has been read. The theme of this anonymous story flows out of a father's lack of influence upon his son that leads to tragic consequences. Dads and moms need to be prepared to be uncomfortable. Our second story, Hans the Crucified, written by our most popular author, Christoph Von Schmid, is a true story that is almost too good to be true. Though not typical of Von Schmid's writings, it is apparent why he wanted children to hear this story of exceptional virtue and courage. The original prefatory remarks will aid you in the historical background that surrounds this dramatic event of the 1600s.

Tom Watkins' Mistake. EMMA LESLIE

In a day of situational ethics, this book will be an excellent opportunity to teach children that one's character is formed by one's obedience to the truth. This story is going to have a significant eternal effect upon many lives.

Nobody Loves Me. O.F. WALTON

O.F. Walton has written much more than a cute children's story. She has reached deeply into the heart and mind of God, bringing light into the darkness of suffering and loneliness. This treasure offers a wonderful training tool to parents and will help children as well as adults realize that in our time of uncertainties, only love never fails.

The Captive. CHRISTOPH VON SCHMID

A gripping account of a sixteen-year-old boy who is captured and enslaved in a foreign country. This story will break down the barriers between cultures, and reveal the true marks of a genuine Christian.

The Bird's Nest. CHRISTOPH VON SCHMID

Strength of character lies in the determination to hold on to truth regardless of circumstances or consequences. The hero in this story proves to us that every seemingly insignificant deed is noticed by God.

The Wide, Wide World. SUSAN WARNER

The first book by an American author to sell one million copies, *The Wide, Wide World* is an endearing novel about a little girl who faces unrelenting affliction, only to be reminded of the One who has charge over her. On a blustery winter day, this is the book to reach for!

Shipwrecked, but not Lost. HON. MRS. DUNDAS

Impulsive, impatient young boys find themselves reaping the dreadful consequences of following foolish counsel. But there *is* a God of mercy who wants to spare his children from shipwreck!

Fireside Readings. VARIOUS AUTHORS

A wonderful collection of 19ᵗʰ century short stories that will give your family hours of enjoyment together. Each story has been carefully selected to challenge, inspire, and give a message of hope. We are pleased to introduce the first volume of our new collection of "*Fireside Readings.*"

Buried in the Snow. FRANZ HOFFMAN

Buried in the Snow, full of twists and turns and unsuspecting dangers, will cause you to see life from a different perspective. You will be blessed by the gentle wisdom of an old grandfather and the unconditional love of his grandson as they come face to face with one of the most difficult decisions of their lives. From the depths of despair to the pinnacle of blessing, this dramatic encounter will surely elicit a full spectrum of emotional responses.

The Wrestler of Philippi. FANNIE E. NEWBERRY.

Here is a story of Rome's staggering contrasts — extreme poverty amidst the wildest extravagance; treacherous dungeon life in darkness and chains amidst the splendors and amusements of luxurious court life. This dramatic unfolding of *The Wrestler of Philippi* will grip your heart as you experience the true test of loyalty and the triumph of faith!

A Puzzling Pair. AMY LEFEUVRE

Inseparable twins, Guy and Berry are bursting with creativity and spunk. They are on a mission...to fill Guy's very big picture of the second coming of Jesus with all the people who are ready to meet Him! But his picture must be true, and time is running out! This rather unique approach to evangelism is as pure, bold, and simple as it gets!

Amy and Her Brothers. ANONYMOUS

In every world-worn man there is a human heart that craves a God to trust, a Christ to lean upon — an unsatisfied heart. In *Amy and Her Brothers* the heartache and innocent faith of an orphan child paints a real-life picture of the hidden suffering all around us, challenging us to be more attentive to the hurts of those nearby.

Sir Knight of the Splendid Way. W.E. CULE

A captivating allegory — a rich literary masterpiece that will encourage any weary traveler. This beautifully-bound work depicts life as a journey, reaching toward a beacon of hope in the City of the Great King. In the midst of conflict, *Sir Knight* will inspire you to press on.

The Beggar's Blessing. MARK HAMBY

A true story from the 1800s about a little girl who sacrificed her savings for a starving beggar. Full-color illustrations will capture the hearts of children as they learn that sacrifice is the cornerstone for surprising blessings. This is a story that you will never forget and is sure to become a children's classic!

Tales of the Kingdom. MAINS

Back in print by popular demand, this allegorical children's classic will take you on a journey to the enchanted city as you relive the wonderful experiences of God's great deliverance. I would place this treasure on an equal with *The Chronicles of Narnia and Pilgrim's Progress.*

The True Princess. ANGELA HUNT

This book is a classic that will teach children what makes a true princess in Jesus' eyes! Truly a treasure to be passed on to the next generation. Based on the Scriptural teachings of servanthood.

Duties of Parents. J.C. RYLE

J. C. Ryle, author of *Thoughts for Young Men*, is no stranger to Lamplighter Publishing. Determined to present a biblically balanced approach to parenting, it is our delight to offer this unique book from the 19th century. What makes this parenting book unique from the rest, is Ryle's ability to candidly express and expose common defects of parenting; and though this book is sure to inflict pain, Ryle also skillfully offers the grace-full balm to heal and restore relationships.

The Education of a Child. FENELON

In all my years of education, I have not come across a more thorough and common sense approach to education than Francois Fenelon's treatise on education during the 17th century. Commissioned to educate King Louis XIV's grandson to prepare him for the throne, Fenelon abandoned all modern approaches to education and followed the genius of the ancient Hebrews, Egyptians, and Greeks. Fenelon believed that the ten classical virtues were the foundation for educational models and could only be taught through friendship and a gentle approach.

The Lamplighter Newsletter

Free and available upon request. Rich with biblical insights on marriage, parenting, book reviews, teaching ideas, mentoring boys and nurturing girls, and a special section devoted to "Let God's Creatures Be the Teachers."

LAMPLIGHTER
PUBLISHING

Books from the Rare Collector's Series can be
purchased in sets of five for a discount. Please call
1-888-246-7735 for pricing information.

P.O. Box 777
Waverly, PA 18471
1-888-A-Gospel

e-mail: info@lamplighterpublishing.com
www.lamplighterpublishing.com

Making ready a people prepared for the Lord.
Luke 1:17